"I Didn't Walk Away From You,"

Kyle said.

"No?" Susan countered. "Well, then, how could you describe what you did? I mean, one minute we were kissing and the next minute—"

"I was running scared."

"*What?* Are you saying you were...afraid?"

"Yes," he said.

"Of what?"

"Of pushing too far, too fast. Of taking too much and giving too little. Of getting things wrong I wanted to get absolutely right."

"And now?" she finally asked.

His gaze never wavered. "I'm still afraid, Susan."

"But you're here."

He stood gazing down at her. Then he raised her hand to his mouth, brushing the knuckles of her fingers with his lips. "There are things stronger than fear," he said huskily. "Feelings like need...and want..."

"You...want me?" she whispered.

"More than anything on earth."

Dear Reader,

November is a time for giving thanks, and this year I have an awful lot to be thankful for—my family, my friends and my terrific job. Because it's through my job that I get to bring to you, the readers, books written by fabulous authors. These are love stories that will give you a lift when you're down, that will make you laugh and cry and rediscover the unique joy of falling in love.

This November has so *many* wonderful stories, starting with the latest in Annette Broadrick's SONS OF TEXAS series, *Marriage Texas Style!* (If you missed the earlier SONS OF TEXAS, don't worry, because this volume also stands alone.)

Next, there's our *Man of the Month* ex-sky jockey Kyle Gordon. Kyle is cocky, opinionated, sexy—altogether he's perfect, and he more than meets his match in schoolteacher Susan Brooks.

November is completed with Barbara Boswell's *Double Trouble* (don't ask me to explain the plot—just read the book), Joan Johnston's *Honey and the Hired Hand,* Doreen Owens Malek's *Arrow in the Snow* (welcome back, Doreen!), and Leslie Davis Guccione's *A Rock and a Hard Place.*

So take time from your busy holiday schedule to curl up with a good Desire book. I know I'm going to!

All the best,

Lucia Macro
Senior Editor

CAROLE BUCK
BLUE SKY GUY

SILHOUETTE *Desire*®
Published by Silhouette Books New York
America's Publisher of Contemporary Romance

SILHOUETTE BOOKS
300 East 42nd St., New York, N.Y. 10017

BLUE SKY GUY

ISBN: 0-373-05750-4

First Silhouette Books printing November 1992

All the characters in this book have no existence outside the imagination of the author and have no relation whatsoever to anyone bearing the same name or names. They are not even distantly inspired by any individual known or unknown to the author, and all incidents are pure invention.

Printed in the U.S.A.

CAROLE BUCK

is a television news writer and movie reviewer who lives in Atlanta. She is single. Her hobbies include cake decorating, ballet and traveling. She collects frogs, but does not kiss them. Carole says she's in love with life; she hopes the books she writes reflect this.

To Lucia Macro
Many thanks. May your skies always be sunny.

One

The alien invasion was getting worse. Much worse.

The evil Embols had armed their troops to the teeth for a final assault. Given that each of these particular troops had six separate sets of fangs, this added up to a whole lot of weapons.

The fate of planet Earth rested in the slightly callused hands of Kyle Lochner Gordon, ex-astronaut and former fearless fighter pilot in the U.S. Air Force. He, and he alone, was the world's last best hope.

It was quite a challenge.

This was just fine with Kyle. What did he care if the odds of victory were a billion—or maybe a zillion—to one and getting higher with each passing second? As long as there was a chance—any chance at all—Kyle was ready to take it.

Arm the weapon.

Acquire the target.

Activate the triggering mechanism.

KA-BOOM!

So far, so good, Kyle decided, assessing the damage he'd just inflicted on the advancing alien horde. It was his not-so-humble opinion that he was doing okay against the extraterrestrial enemy, all things considered.

Of course the brown-haired, bespectacled ten-year-old boy crowding his right elbow at the control console obviously rated his performance much better than okay. Kyle was well aware that the kid—Charles Michael Brooks by birth, just plain Charlie by choice—was awed by his video-game virtuosity.

"Wow!" Charlie gasped ecstatically as Kyle blew one of the Embols' transport ships to smithereens. A multicolored explosion lit up the video screen, accompanied by a series of electronically generated sound effects. The computerized scorekeeper added a slew of points to an already impressive tally.

Kyle dismissed the shot with a shrug. He played it cool, allowing himself only a brief smile of satisfaction. He had a certain image to uphold.

"Jeez! There's another one!" Charlie yelped. "Get it, Kyle!"

Ready. Aim. Fire.

KA-BLOOEY!

Another ten thousand or so Embols were reduced to space dust.

Hot dog! a voice inside Kyle's skull declared.

Kyle tensed. He'd been hearing this particular voice a lot lately. He hadn't yet figured out its source. If it belonged to his conscience, it had picked a lousy time to start trying to influence his behavior.

So? Kyle countered, manipulating the computer game's joystick. He thumbed the firing button. The video screen produced another violently colored light show. I'm good enough to get away with it.

Maybe once. The response was quick and cut to the bone. *But not anymore.*

And then, without warning, it happened.

The sickeningly familiar wave of dizziness and disorientation. The sudden blurring of his vision. The high-pitched ringing in his ears. Kyle's concentration cracked like an eggshell in a vice. His stomach started to rebel. A sour taste flooded his tongue.

The floor in the arcade seemed to tilt. Kyle felt himself sway. Maintaining his equilibrium ceased to be an easily achievable option. His fingers—once so sure, once so steady—spasmed involuntarily against the slick plastic surface of the video game console.

Kyle squeezed his eyelids shut, struggling for control. Dammit, he swore under his breath. Dammit! The doctors had said this wouldn't happen as long as he took his medication as prescribed and kept his feet planted firmly on the ground.

heard Charlie gasp in horror. The sound seemed distant though reaching him from across a great distance.

pened his eyes. He couldn't see, much less think,

n!" Charlie urged with bloodthirsty zeal, apparous to Kyle's distress. "Get 'em!"

g on his instincts, Kyle did just that. He got 'em.

A split second later, trying to battle back a soul-savaging sense of uselessness, he got 'em some more.

"Awesome!" Charlie practically swooned with excitement.

The arcade floor stabilized. Kyle's wooziness receded like an outgoing tide. His vision cleared and his ears stopped ringing. His fingers returned to operating on command.

Better, he told himself. Much better. All conditions: A-OK.

"Megadeath to the Embols!" his preteen companion crowed.

Deep down, Kyle was naggingly aware that he probably was deriving a tad too much pleasure from Charlie's unbridled admiration. Absorbing a bit of hero worship was one thing. Marinating in it and begging for more was entirely another.

Hot dog! the voice inside his skull opined once again.

Shut up! Kyle ordered sharply.

Who said a thirty-six-year-old man on the verge of saving humankind wasn't entitled to a little appreciation? he demanded of himself as he deftly detonated a series of radiation bombs. Just where was it written that heroes had to be self-effacing, huh? Some of the gutsiest guys he knew were applause-addicted goofballs.

Ready.

Aim.

F-i-r-e.

Megadeath to more Embols. Rack up another big bunch of points.

Besides, Kyle went on silently, performing a swift series of evasive maneuvers, he'd taken quite a hammering recently. He'd had his life turned upside down and he was hurting. If the adulation of a space-crazy ten-year-old helped to ease his pain, he wasn't about to—

"Uh-oh."

The two-syllable exclamation was soft, yet it slamme through Kyle's cocoon of self-absorption like a fist cerned, he slanted a glance at Charlie.

The kid was looking toward the entrance of the ar hazel eyes were round and wide behind his wire-fram The expression on his freckled face held a mixture and guilt.

Kyle experienced an odd tightening in his belly. He tra the line of Charlie's gaze with his own. What the . . . ?

He spotted the answer before he finished formulating the question.

"It's my mom," Charlie announced with a tinge of trepidation.

Kyle's throat seemed to close up. He swallowed hard, trying not to stare at the dark-haired, dark-eyed woman who was heading toward them with a gracefully determined stride.

"Yeah, kid," he responded without inflection. "I know."

Man, did he ever.

The woman moving in their direction was Susan Brooks. Susan Eleanor Brooks. She was "Mom" to her only child, Charlie. She'd been "Suzie" and "sweetheart" to her late husband, Mike.

And to Kyle . . .

She was everything he'd ever wanted.

Kyle recoiled from this unbidden thought as though it were a rattlesnake. Where the hell had that notion come from? he asked himself furiously. Susan Brooks was nothing to him. *Nothing!*

Kyle dragged his gaze back to the video screen. It took him a moment to register the meaning of the two words flashing there.

GAME OVER.

Rough translation: planet Earth had been conquered by the evil Embols and it was all his fault.

The game was *over*. Finished. Just like a lot of other things. Like his career. Like his chance of fulfilling the dream he'd cherished for three decades. Like his whole damned—

Kyle slammed the brakes on this train of thought. He den it to the end of the line more often than he cared to during the past few weeks. The trip was a downward spir ultimate destination was despair.

He glared at the blinking video screen in front o struggling with a desire to hit something. He'd had to c with this kind of need a lot lately. The one time he' cumbed to it, he'd bruised his knuckles so badly he hadn able to make a fist for three days. The wall he'd taken a at hadn't even sustained a minor dent.

Kyle lifted his head and looked back at Susan. He couldn't help himself. He couldn't do much about the sudden stiffening in his groin, either, except hope the zipper of his jeans would hold.

All right. All right! He'd admit it. Susan Brooks was… something to him. But exactly what that something was, he didn't know.

It was crazy, of course. The way he was feeling was stark raving nuts! He'd only had two real encounters with this woman in his entire life. The first had been roughly eleven years before, at a wedding. The second had taken place about nine years later, at a funeral.

Two meetings, at opposite ends of the emotional spectrum. Yet on both occasions, the response Susan Eleanor Brooks had evoked in him had been the same. It had been potent to the point of being physically painful. It had also been utterly inappropriate.

A man wasn't supposed to lust after the newly wed wife of his best buddy from childhood. Yet Kyle knew he had.

And when that best buddy died, transforming his wife into a heartbroken widow, a man wasn't supposed to lust after her, either. Yet Kyle was bitterly conscious he'd done that, as well.

The surge of attraction he'd felt during his first face-to-face encounter with Susan had shocked him. White-lace dresses and orange-blossom bouquets—to say nothing of solemn pledges of eternal devotion—had always been rock-bottom low on his list of sexual turn-ons. Nonetheless, he'd taken one look at Mike Brooks's bride and *whammo.* White-lace dresses and orange-blossom bouquets had suddenly seemed like the ultimate in aphrodisiacs.

As for the surge of attraction he'd experienced during his second meeting with Susan . . .

That had shamed him. It had shamed him when it had happened and it shamed him now, more than two years after the fact.

Kyle sucked in a breath. She doesn't know, he reminded himself. You made sure of that. *Nobody* knows. And they wouldn't believe it if you testified to it on a stack of Bibles. The Supersonic Stud and the Happy Homemaker? Oh, sure. You don't believe it yourself, and you're the one who's got the eleven-year-old urge to merge with the lady!

He'd realized he'd be seeing her again, of course. His decision to spend some time in Wilder's Forge while he tried to figure out what to do with his life had made that inevitable. Wilder's Forge, New York, was the kind of small town where everybody, sooner or later, wound up seeing everybody else.

In a way, Kyle was surprised he and Susan hadn't run into each other before this. His acquaintanceship with Charlie Brooks was nearly two weeks old and he'd figured . . . Well, no, he hadn't *figured* at all. That made it sound as though he'd been using the son to get to the mother. And he hadn't been. He genuinely enjoyed hanging out with Charlie.

"Uh . . . hi, Mom. Did you get your car fixed?"

The sound of Charlie's voice yanked Kyle back into the present. Susan Brooks had come to a halt next to the video game he'd been playing.

She was near enough for him to catch the fresh floral scent of her perfume. Near enough so he could see the delicate tracery of laugh lines at the outer corners of her long-lashed brown eyes. Near enough so he could reach out and touch her if he chose to.

He did not choose to. He chose to jam his hands into the pockets of his jeans, instead.

If Susan was conscious of his proximity, Kyle could see no sign of it. She appeared to be oblivious to everything except her son.

"Appeared" was the operative word, Kyle decided after a moment. There was no way the awareness he was experiencing could be entirely one-sided. Susan's apparent indifference to his existence had to be feigned. She knew he was standing there, expecting to be acknowledged. He *knew* she knew it!

"Yes, I got my car fixed," Susan said. "And I've been out front sitting in it, waiting for you for more than twenty minutes, young man."

"Well, uh, I kinda got, uh, uh—"

"Don't blame him, Susan," Kyle interrupted. It was a bid for attention. He wouldn't deny that. But it was also an attempt to bail Charlie out of trouble. The kid was a buddy. And according to his code, buddies ran interference for each other when the going got tough. "I'm the one at fault."

Susan looked at him. Coolly. Questioningly. He responded automatically, flashing the smile that more than one of his former lady friends had accused him of practicing in front of a mirror when no one was looking. He didn't, of course. Practice smiling in front of a mirror, that is. He'd never felt the need to. The Gordon Grin, as it had been dubbed in his high-school yearbook, had been programmed into his genes. Sure, he'd... refined his use of the expression over time. He'd have been a fool not to. But he'd never stooped to rehearsing the basic technique.

"Oh?" Susan said.

Kyle was stunned. While he'd been given the brush-off a few times in his life, he'd never before been reduced to feeling like a piece of human lint. Susan Brooks had done it with a single syllable.

That's it? he wondered after a second or two.

That's it, the voice inside his skull affirmed with malicious cheerfulness. *The Supersonic Stud crashes and burns.*

Kyle spent a moment wondering if his use of Susan's first name had been a tactical error. Maybe she'd been offended by the familiarity, he theorized. But, dammit, that's how he'd spent the past eleven years thinking of her! As *Susan!*

Then a series of ego-grinding possibilities occurred to him. What if her indifference hadn't been feigned? What if his response to her was truly unreciprocated? *What if she didn't even remember who he was?*

"Kyle," he supplied tightly. He yanked his right hand out of his jeans pocket and extended it. He tried flashing the smile again. For the first time in his life, it felt absolutely phony. "Kyle Gordon."

After a fractional hesitation, Susan clasped his right hand with her own. Yet Kyle felt the brief contact in every fiber of his body.

"Yes," Susan replied, disengaging her fingers from his. "I know."

Kyle caught a glimpse of something in her eyes then. It came and went so quickly, and was so wholly at odds with the aloofness of her manner, that he couldn't begin to put a name to it. He couldn't even be certain it wasn't a product of his own overheated imagination.

"You...know?" he echoed.

"'Course she knows," Charlie asserted. "You're famous, Kyle."

Famous as a has-been, the voice inside Kyle's skull corrected.

"Captain Gordon, Charlie," said Susan.

"Huh?"

No, the voice went on. *You're not even that, are you? You're a barely-were and a never-will-be-again.*

"Captain Gordon," Susan repeated firmly. "Not Kyle."

"But—"

"Actually," Kyle cut in, "it's Major."

Susan's gaze collided with his. Again he saw a flash of something in the depths of her dark brown eyes. It was the same something he'd glimpsed before. He still didn't know how to interpret it, but he no longer questioned whether it was really there.

"Excuse me?" Susan asked, an odd little catch in her voice.

"I was promoted to Major about eighteen months ago," he explained.

Not that it makes one damned bit of difference now, the relentless voice pointed out.

"I *told* you that, Mom," Charlie said with an edge of exasperation. "Don't you *remember?*"

Susan gave her son a sharp look. "About as well as you remembered I told you to meet me in front of this place at noon."

Charlie grimaced, clearly regretting having spoken up. "I'm sorry," he apologized quickly. "I didn't mean to forget. It wasn't on purpose. Honest! But things just...just kind of happened, you know? First I had this seriously outstanding run on Planet Killer. My best score ever. Then I met up with, uh, uh..."

"Kyle," Kyle filled in.

"Kyle!" Susan protested, then flushed as though she'd said something she shouldn't have. She gestured. "I mean—"

"Kyle," Kyle insisted, taking advantage of her momentary loss of poise. "I'm not entitled to the Major anymore. And the only Mr. Gordon in Wilder's Forge is my uncle, H.G. So, please—" he deliberately waited a beat "—Susan. Call me Kyle."

He watched the color in Susan's heart-shaped face intensify. She'd blushed at her wedding reception, too, he suddenly remembered. He'd taken her hand when they'd been introduced during the receiving line and she'd blushed.

He'd never really wondered why—until now.

"Susan?" he pressed.

At six feet, he was a head taller than she was. She had to tilt her chin up to look directly into his eyes. She'd seemed reluctant to meet his gaze eleven years before, he recalled.

A second or so of silence passed. Then Susan conceded his point.

"Kyle," she said.

There was another brief pause. Kyle shifted his weight, uncomfortably conscious of a renewed throbbing between his thighs.

"Hey, uh, Kyle?"

Kyle looked at Charlie, grateful for the distraction. "Hey, uh, what?"

"You want to have lunch with us? We're going to Fiori's to get pizza."

Susan made a noise that was somewhere between a choke and a gasp. Kyle was certain the sound was not meant as an endorsement of her son's invitation.

"You *promised* we could get pizza, Mom," Charlie said, turning. He surveyed his mother's expression. The smooth skin of his forehead pleated. He lowered his head and hunched his shoulders. "You're not going to make me *starve* or eat *salad* just because I forgot to meet you out front, are you?" he asked pathetically. "I said I was sorry."

Good performance, Charlie, Kyle thought, forcing himself to swallow a laugh.

Charlie's mother did not seem so appreciative.

"Oh, for heaven's sake, Charlie!" Susan snapped. "No, I'm not going to make you starve or—God forbid—eat salad just because you forgot to meet me out front."

"So..." the boy said with a hint of wheedling, "does that mean we can get pizza?"

A sigh of maternal resignation. "Yes. That means we can get pizza."

"Pepperoni?"

"Whatever."

"Kyle, too?"

Kyle knew Susan was looking at him. He could feel the touch of her gaze. After a few moments, he turned his head and looked back at her.

"Kyle, too," she agreed with obvious reluctance. "If he wants."

He did. He most definitely did.

Do you have any idea how boring it is listening to someone talk about things he used to do? the voice inside Kyle's skull inquired trenchantly as he drove home from Fiori's Pizza Palace several hours later.

Charlie was interested, Kyle countered, exerting a tad more pressure on the gas pedal.

Susan wasn't.

You don't have a clue about what interests Susan Brooks.

You do?

Look, why don't you get off my back?

Why don't you get a life?

I had one, dammit!

So? Get another!

Doing what?

Kyle cut the steering wheel sharply, turning onto the narrow road that led to his uncle's house. His car lurched, its suspension system groaning in protest. He was driving faster than he should have been, and he knew it. But he needed the speed. He craved the communion between man and machine.

Maybe you could join the demolition derby. The sardonic proposal coincided with a bone-jarring dip in the road.

"Yeah, right," Kyle muttered, easing up on the gas pedal. No point in abusing automotive history, he told himself. And the car he was driving was precisely that. It was a Detroit dinosaur: a big, boxy, raging-red Thunderbird convertible, complete with tail fins and a ton of chrome trim. He'd bought it, secondhand, in high school and spent months restoring it.

He'd had some of his best times on Earth behind the wheel of this car, Kyle acknowledged, smiling just a little. And—he glanced at the reflection in the rearview mirror—he'd chalked up a few extremely memorable episodes in its vinyl-covered back seat, too.

Maybe Susan would be interested in hearing about them, his oh-so-helpful inner voice suggested.

Shut up! Kyle ordered, shifting gears. Just . . . shut up.

Remarkably, the voice obeyed.

The voice hadn't said much during lunch. That had suited Kyle just fine. Unfortunately, Susan had been equally reticent, which had irritated the hell out of him.

He'd tried to get her to talk to him, but he hadn't been able to come up with the right conversational bait. He'd found himself rejecting most of his usual opening lines and icebreakers. The few he *had* deemed worthy of uttering had elicited polite responses and nothing more.

Even the Gordon Grin had failed him.

All of which was not to imply that he, Susan and Charlie had chowed down on a jumbo pepperoni pizza in silence. The kid had chattered throughout the entire meal, proclaiming that he could hardly wait for the start of summer vacation and predicting that the two-week science camp he had been selected to attend would be the greatest experience of his life.

Their meal had also been punctuated by the drop-in appearances of a number of Susan's acquaintances. Among them, a blond beautician named Wendy Marino. To say Ms. Marino was ''built'' would have been an understatement. From what he'd seen—and heaven knew, she'd certainly had herself on display—the lady in question was prime centerfold material.

That Charlie would get around to the subject of flying had been inevitable. Unavoidable. Not that Kyle hadn't tried to deflect the boy's inquiries about his career as a pilot. He had. In fact, now that he thought about it, he had the distinct impression that Susan had attempted to shift her son away from the subject, too. But Charlie had been locked on target and he wouldn't be shaken off. Eventually Kyle had begun answering his questions.

Kyle turned into his uncle's gravel-covered driveway. The car's whitewall tires spewed up a spray of small stones as he made the maneuver. He brought his car to a halt inside the garage that was one of a series of additions that had been built onto his uncle's house. The most recent of these additions was an antenna-topped observatory. The tower-shaped structure was a tribute to the size of Horace George ''H.G.'' Gordon's royalty checks and to the intensity of his commitment to SETI—the Search for Extraterrestrial Intelligence.

Maybe he *had* gotten carried away with his fearless-flier routine during lunch, Kyle admitted, shutting off the engine and getting out of the car. Still, it had felt so natural to talk about flying. He'd been bitten by the wild-blue-yonder bug more than thirty years before. The fever was in his blood. Having his wings permanently clipped wasn't going to cure it.

The psychiatrist he'd been ordered to talk to after the final verdict on his medical condition had come in had warned him he'd probably require a "period of adjustment" following his discharge from the service. Of course the shrink hadn't been able to predict how long this period was going to last nor advise what kind of adjustment ought to be made during it. He'd just wanted to offer Kyle some "insight" into what might lie ahead.

Kyle hadn't needed any insight into his future once he'd heard he was being washed out on a disability. He'd known exactly what lay ahead. That was one of the reasons he'd started a punching match with a wall.

"Anybody home?" Kyle called as he let himself into his uncle's house. H. G. Gordon believed passionately in a great many things, including the inviolability of the First Amendment, the existence of UFOs and the inherent superiority of crunchy peanut butter over smooth. He did not, however, believe in locking doors. Kyle had taxed the older man about this on a number of occasions, but to no avail.

"In my office!" a hearty male voice responded from the back of the house.

H.G.'s "office" was a large, skylighted room lined floor to ceiling with books and crammed with every kind of office equipment known to man. During its periods of maximum tidiness, the place looked as though it had been professionally ransacked. At the moment, however, it was merely a total mess. And kneeling in the middle of the total mess, surrounded by a dozen or so tape-sealed cardboard cartons, was Horace George Gordon.

Horace George Gordon, the man who'd made himself rich and famous writing the kind of science fiction he liked to read. Horace George Gordon, the man who'd adopted the orphaned six-year-old son of his only brother and raised him as his own.

H.G. was short, stout and silver-haired. He had a ruddy complexion and beaming blue eyes. Young children occasionally confused him with Santa Claus. Kyle thought the mix-up was quite understandable.

"Looking for something specific, H.G.?" he asked, taking off the aviator-style sunglasses he'd been wearing and hanging them from one of the belt loops on his jeans.

His uncle paused in the act of slicing through the tape on one of the cardboard cartons with a carving knife. "Oh, no. No," he said, shaking his head. "I just got this sudden urge to look through some of the boxes I've had stored up in the attic. I think a lot of the stuff is yours."

"I see," Kyle responded mildly, advancing into the room. "I don't suppose this 'sudden urge' has anything to do with the fact that you've got a book due before the end of the summer?" While his uncle was a remarkably prolific writer, he was also a world-class procrastinator.

H.G. produced his own version of the Gordon Grin. "Absolutely nothing," he declared with palpable falsity. He returned to dissecting the carton. "Are you hungry?" he inquired after a few moments. "It's a little late for lunch, but I've got—"

"I ate, thanks."

The older man looked up again. "Alone?"

"I had a pizza with, uh, Charlie," Kyle answered. He felt curiously reluctant to mention the name of his other dining companion.

"Charlie?" H.G.'s marshmallow-puffy eyebrows lifted for an instant, then settled back into place. "Oh, yes. Charlie Brooks. You've been spending a fair amount of time with him, haven't you?"

Kyle's mind flashed back to his initial meeting with Charlie. It had happened at the local library. He'd gone there to return some books for his uncle. It should have been an easy errand. Unfortunately, several of the volumes involved had turned out to be long overdue. It had taken the librarian nearly five minutes to calculate the fine.

He'd just finished shelling out the required amount of cash when someone behind him had said, "Uh . . . 'scuse me."

He'd pivoted and found himself facing a skinny, book-toting young boy. A stranger. And yet not a stranger. Something about the kid had triggered a peculiar tremor of recognition deep within Kyle.

"'Scuse me," the youngster had repeated, his voice breath-less, his hazel eyes very bright. "You're Kyle Gordon, aren't you? Major Kyle Gordon?"

The boy had pronounced Kyle's name and rank with a re-spectfulness that bordered on awe. He'd sounded as though he wasn't certain whether he was worthy of speaking them aloud.

"Yeah, that's right," Kyle had affirmed after a second. He'd gotten a momentary kick out of the kid's attitude. But the kick had been followed by a brutal crash. Because he'd known damned well he wasn't the "Major Kyle Gordon" the boy be-lieved him to be. At least, not anymore.

The youngster's freckled face had lit up. "Oh, wow!" he'd exclaimed. "I knew it was you. I knew it! I heard you were back in Wilder's Forge. You used to be friends with my dad. I'm Charlie. Charlie Brooks."

Kyle's previous tremor of recognition had erupted into a full-scale quake of comprehension.

Brooks. Mike's son, he'd realized.

And . . . Susan's, he'd amended a heartbeat later.

"Kyle?" H.G. prompted.

Kyle returned to the present with a start.

"Yeah, I've spent some time with Charlie," he told his un-cle, hoping he didn't sound as defensive as he suddenly felt. "Why not? He's Mike Brooks's son. Mike was my best friend when I was growing up, remember?"

"Of course I remember," H.G. replied. He set down the knife and began folding back the flaps of the carton.

There was a short silence. Kyle ran a hand through his light brown hair. It was a little strange to feel something more than stubble against his palm when he did so. He'd worn his hair clipped high and tight from the time he'd entered the Air Force Academy. He'd decided to let it grow out after he'd returned to Wilder's Forge—part of his "period of adjustment."

Susan had let her hair grow out, too, he reflected tangen-tially. It had been chopped off at chin length, hanging limp and lank around her pale, hollow-cheeked face when he'd seen her at Mike's funeral. Today it tumbled to her shoulders in glossy mink-brown curls.

"I admire Susan," his uncle commented casually, rooting around inside the now opened carton.

Kyle snapped to attention. "What?"

H.G. pulled some items out of the box, examined them curiously, then tossed them aside. "Susan Brooks," he said. "I admire her."

Kyle wasn't certain how to respond. "I didn't realize you knew her."

"Oh, yes. I've spoken to several of her classes." The older man stopped rummaging and sat back on his heels. He cocked his head. "She teaches English at the high school, you know."

Kyle nodded. "Uh, yeah. Charlie's mentioned that."

"Ah. I see."

What was that supposed to mean? Kyle wondered irritably. Was H.G. implying that he'd been pumping Charlie for information about Susan? Well, he hadn't been! Okay. Okay. Maybe he'd asked the kid a question or two or three, but that had been the extent of it.

Kyle stared at his uncle, who'd returned to taking things out of the carton. Then, goaded by an emotion he couldn't identify, he stepped over one box, skirted two others and hunkered down next to the older man. "She was there, too," he admitted abruptly.

H.G. turned his head, blinking owlishly. "Who?"

"Susan. Susan Brooks."

"Oh."

"At lunch."

"Ah. The pizza. With young Charlie."

"Yeah." Kyle picked up the carving knife. Frowning, he prepared to do battle with one of the boxes. "I don't think Susan likes me very much."

His uncle did not try to argue the point.

Neither did the voice inside his skull.

Two

She didn't like him.

After substantial consideration, Susan Eleanor Brooks had decided that her apparently complicated feelings about Kyle Lochner Gordon boiled down to this one uncomplicated truth.

She didn't like him!

And yet she couldn't stop thinking about the man. She'd tried, but she couldn't. Which wasn't to suggest that there was anything pleasant about her thoughts, she assured herself, trying to keep the situation in perspective. Indeed not. Everything she thought about Kyle Lochner was awful.

Well, actually, no, her fundamental integrity forced her to amend after a moment. Not quite *everything* everything. *Almost* everything.

Grimacing, Susan reached for one of the dozens of forms she had to complete before the close of the school year, just four days away. "No more pencils, no more books..." she muttered, invoking the traditional start-of-summer-vacation chant as she scanned the document, ticked off the appropriate spaces and signed her name at the bottom. She put the photocopied sheet on top of the stack of similar papers piled tidily on the right side of her desk.

She ran an assessing eye around her classroom. Maybe she should take a crack at her requisite end-of-the-year inventory of supplies, she thought. That certainly would keep her mind off... ah... whatever.

She glanced at her wristwatch. It was now three-forty. She was due to pick Charlie up from a Boy Scout meeting at four-thirty. Hmm...

No. Not enough time, Susan decided. Although the drive to the site of the Scout meeting wouldn't take more than a few minutes, there was no telling how long she might need to cajole her car into starting. Despite the repair work it had undergone on Saturday, it had exhibited a fair degree of automotive temperament this morning.

So. Back to the paperwork. And to thinking about Kyle Gordon.

She'd *never* liked him. Even before she'd met him face-to-face, she'd heard enough about Kyle Lochner Gordon to know him for what he was. And what he was, was a cocky, skirt-chasing, bend-the-rules playboy.

She still had great difficulty accepting that Mike, her calm and quiet and stable and sensible Mike, had considered Kyle his "best buddy." He'd claimed to admire him. To envy him, even.

Lord...when she recalled the stories Mike had told her about the stunts he and his best buddy had pulled as they were growing up in Wilder's Forge! Kyle had always been the instigator of their adventures, of course. He'd recklessly led. Mike had aided, abetted and loyally followed.

"I wanted to be like him, Suzie," Mike had confessed to her late one night as she'd sat by his hospital bed holding his hand. His raspy voice had been full of wry amusement. His jaundiced hazel eyes had glinted with happy memories. "I wanted to be just like Kyle."

Susan sighed. First Mike, she thought resentfully. And now Mike's son.

She'd picked up a hint of hero worship two weeks before, when Charlie had come home and excitedly announced that he'd talked to Kyle Gordon. While she'd experienced a tremor of dismay at the news, she hadn't had the heart to quash his enthusiasm. She'd reminded herself that Charlie had reached the age when it was natural for him to seek strong male role models. Although Kyle was not the role model she would have chosen, she'd understood his appeal.

Charlie's fascination with his late father's friend had become increasingly obvious during the days that followed his initial announcement. But it wasn't until Susan had seen his hanging-on-every-word demeanor at Fiori's Pizza Palace that she'd realized exactly how much he'd—

"So, Susan," a brisk feminine voice said. "What's this I hear about you and Kyle Gordon?"

Startled, Susan nearly sent the stack of forms toppling off her desk and onto the floor. She looked to her left. Standing in the classroom doorway was Ramona Bozeman.

Ramona Bozeman had graduated from Wilder's Forge High School the same year Mike and Kyle had. She was now the school's guidance counselor. The forthright and funny mother of fifteen-year-old twin girls, DeeDee and LouAnne, she was one of Susan's closest friends.

"Uh, I don't know, Ramona," Susan answered, gathering the scattered papers back into a pile. Her hands weren't entirely steady as she went about the task. Neither was her pulse. She did, however, manage to keep her tone even. "What do you hear?"

Ramona ambled into the classroom. "That you and he had lunch on Saturday," she replied. She made "lunch" sound as though it was an illicit activity. An illicit activity of which she thoroughly approved.

Susan rolled her eyes. "Did you also hear that this lunch was a pepperoni pizza at Fiori's and that Charlie ate most of it?"

Ramona made an airy gesture, clearly communicating that she was more interested in the spirit of the tête-à-tête than the specifics of it. She perched herself on the edge of Susan's desk and waited.

"Just where did you hear about . . . us?" Susan inquired after a few moments, feigning great interest in seeing that the papers on her desk were arranged just so. She wasn't surprised that her friend had gotten wind of Saturday's encounter. As she was well aware, Wilder's Forge was the kind of place where everybody knew everybody else's business. She'd been greeted by at least four female acquaintances while she'd been in the pizza restaurant. First and foremost had been Wendy Marino, owner of the Curl Up and Dye Style Salon and the area's most "active" divorcée.

Kyle's presence hadn't exactly passed unnoticed, either. As a matter of fact, Susan was pretty certain that he, not she, had been the reason her friends had decided they'd absolutely *had* to drop by her table and say hello to her. In the case of Wendy Marino, she was positive he'd been the draw. She was also ready to swear he'd relished every second of the beautician's flirtatious attentions.

"Jack spotted you in Fiori's parking lot."

Jack, Susan realized, had to be Jack Wiley, Ramona's older and unmarried brother. He was also the principal of Charlie's school. While Susan did not know him well, she had the impression he was a nice man. Less outgoing and more conservative than his sister perhaps, but nice nonetheless.

"Oh," she responded after a pause.

"That's all?" Ramona asked. "Just 'oh'?"

"What else do you want, Ramona?"

"Have you got something going with Kyle?"

"No! Of course not."

Ramona cocked her head. "Why 'of course not'?"

"Because the idea of my having something going with Kyle Gordon is . . ." Susan gestured, searching for the right adjective. "It's ridiculous, Ramona. I didn't want to have lunch with him. It was all Charlie's idea. He thinks Kyle is the greatest thing since the invention of the computer."

"But you don't."

"I didn't say that."

"You didn't *not* say it, either."

Susan began fiddling with the stack of forms once again.

"Susan?" Ramona probed.

Susan continued shuffling papers. "He makes me . . . uncomfortable."

"Is that uncomfortable bad or uncomfortable good?"

Susan slapped down the documents and gave her friend a sharp look. "Just uncomfortable, all right? *Very* uncomfortable!"

Susan averted her gaze. She didn't want to discuss her feelings about Kyle Gordon with anyone. They were too personal.

She took a deep breath, trying to dam up a sudden wave of remembrance. Her efforts were futile. The past came flooding back.

Her wedding day, more than eleven years before.

She'd been twenty-one and deeply in love with her new husband. Yet she'd taken one look at his best buddy and experienced a surge of attraction so intense that her knees had nearly buckled beneath her.

She'd never felt anything as powerful—nor as primitive—in her life. Certainly not in relation to Mike. While she and he had become lovers shortly after they'd announced their engagement, their physical intimacy had never been the stuff of steamy movie scenes. The pleasure they'd shared had always been a matter of warmth and affection, not wild eroticism.

Susan had come to her wedding day believing that her nature was simply not a strongly sexual one. She'd been totally unprepared for the wanton response Kyle Gordon had evoked in her.

She'd been trembling, her heart hammering inside her satin-and-lace-covered breast, when Mike had performed the necessary receiving-line introductions. Kyle had stepped in front of her, impeccably groomed from the toes of his spit-polished shoes to the top of his short-haired head. He'd looked like a candidate for a military recruiting poster. His squared-shoulder bearing had been assured to the point of arrogance, and there had been a hint of macho swagger in the way he moved.

He hadn't smiled at her. Indeed, his tanned, strong-featured face had been virtually expressionless as he'd taken her right hand with his own and smoothly acknowledged her new status as Mike's wife. The look in his brilliant blue eyes had been utterly unreadable.

She'd gotten no hint that anyone had sensed her response to Kyle—certainly not from him and definitely not from Mike. For this Susan had been deeply grateful. The possibility that another person might ferret out her shameful reaction had filled her with dread.

Yet even as she'd been thanking heaven for everyone's apparent lack of perception, she'd been conscious of an angry jab of resentment at Kyle's seeming obliviousness. Doesn't he feel anything? she'd wondered, acutely aware that her cheeks were aflame. Is he so insensitive he doesn't realize what he's doing to me? Or is he so accustomed to women falling all over him that he takes it as his due—even from his best friend's bride?

While the reception-line encounter hadn't ruined Susan's wedding day, it had irreparably tainted her memory of what should have been a perfect and pristine occasion. And although it hadn't shaken her loving relationship with her husband in any fundamental way, it had planted a nasty nagging question about whether there was a need within her—a need she'd never been conscious of until meeting Kyle—that Mike couldn't fulfill.

Over the nine years of her very happy marriage, Susan had learned to box up her feelings about Kyle Gordon and shove them into the darkest most distant corner of her mind. She'd also managed to avoid any personal contact with him during the few visits he'd made to Wilder's Forge.

And then . . .

Susan closed her eyes for a moment. She didn't want to remember. She didn't!

But she couldn't stop herself from doing so. The memory of what had happened roughly two years and one month earlier was just too strong.

Mike had died of cancer and Kyle had come to his funeral.

He'd been full of anguish. Susan would give him that. Kyle Gordon had been grief stricken about the death of his best buddy.

Yet he'd also been handsome and healthy, and so damnably *alive!*

Susan had hated him for that. And she'd hated herself for being so aware of it. To see Kyle, to sense the virility and vitality in him, had meant being reminded, in the cruelest possible way, of Mike's passing.

Look at me, something about Kyle had seemed to shout at her. *Look at me, Susan! I'm alive and your husband's not.*

And there'd been something worse. Much worse.

Mike's death had left Susan numb inside. Even when she'd been with Charlie, she hadn't been able to feel anything. It had been as though she'd been disconnected from life. If truth be told, she'd welcomed the numbness. The disconnection.

But then she'd seen Kyle at the funeral and her ability to feel had been regenerated, reborn. His compelling presence had forced her to acknowledge that she was as alive as he was.

She'd responded to him. Heaven knew, she hadn't wanted to, but she had. She, Susan Eleanor Brooks, had responded to Kyle Lochner Gordon at the most basic of human levels. She'd responded to him as a woman responds to—

"There's no need to feel guilty, you know."

The sound of Ramona's voice hauled Susan back to the present. She felt a pricking at the inner corners of her eyes and blinked. Glancing down, she saw that her hands were shaking. She clasped them together.

Finally she looked at Ramona. The expression on her friend's round, olive-skinned face held concern and compassion. Susan tried to school her own features into a calm expression but had no idea whether or not her effort succeeded.

"W-what did you say?" she asked.

Ramona leaned forward. "Mike's been dead for more than two years, Susan," she said gently. "I know how much you loved him. I know how deeply you've mourned for him. But life goes on. There's no need for you to feel guilty if you're attracted to Kyle Gordon."

Susan nearly choked. "I am *not* attracted to Kyle Gordon!"

Ramona seemed genuinely taken aback by her vehemence. A line from Shakespeare—"The lady doth protest too much, methinks"—flitted through Susan's brain. She swatted it away.

"Really?" Ramona responded mildly after a few moments. "Well, then, you may be the only female in Wilder's Forge who's out of grade school and not in a nursing home who isn't. I mean—" the corners of her mouth twisted as though she was remembering something amusing "—the man is a total babe."

Susan knew she shouldn't pursue the description, but she couldn't quite put the brakes on. "A . . . total babe?"

Ramona nodded, her lips quirking once again. "Or so DeeDee tells me. The twins saw Kyle last week. They recognized him from the photograph in that Alumni Achievers display here at the high school. He was out jogging. You know. Tank top. Short shorts. Muscles and sweat."

Susan got the picture. She shifted in her seat and crossed her legs. "I take it LouAnne wasn't as impressed with Kyle's looks as her sister was."

"Actually, she called him a stud muffin."

"I . . . see." Susan shifted her position again.

"Oh, come on, Suze." Ramona's tone was teasing, very girl-to-girl. It invited the kind of feminine confessions usually reserved for pajama parties and whispered conversations in ladies' rest rooms. "Are you going to sit there and pretend you don't think Kyle Gordon is a hunk?"

Susan picked up a pen and prepared to return to her paperwork. She hoped Ramona would take the hint and go away. "I really haven't paid that much attention to the man's looks," she said, selecting a form and beginning to fill it out.

"You *must* have noticed his body."

Susan's memory kicked into overdrive, serving up some very specific details about the anatomy of the man she'd lunched with so reluctantly two days before.

Broad shoulders. A classically proportioned chest and torso. A flat stomach. Tautly powerful, denim-clad thighs and long lean legs. Not an ounce of superfluous fat visible anywhere, including that tight little—

"I've noticed he's in good shape," she conceded ungraciously, staring at the form in front of her, willing it to fill her brain. "There's no surprise in that. He was in the military. The military doesn't let its men go around with paunches and bad posture."

"What about his smile?"

"What about it?"

"For heaven's sake, Susan! Kyle Gordon has a killer grin!"

More memories.

The sudden undeniably seductive curving of a pair of sensually shaped lips. Deeply grooved dimples revealing themselves. Strong, even teeth flashing white against suntanned skin.

"I think Mike said he wore braces," Susan lied. She knew her husband had been the one who'd had to wear braces. And glasses. His best buddy had been endowed with perfectly straight pearly whites as well as twenty-twenty vision.

Susan scribbled a dozen or so words on the form. The words were supposed to make a complete, coherent sentence. While she had some serious doubts about whether they actually did, she did not go back and check.

"And then there are those gorgeous green eyes of his," Ramona observed with a swoony little sigh.

"Blue," Susan corrected, then winced when she realized what she'd done. Angered, she looked up. Her friend's expression was smug.

"You're right," Ramona told her. "They *are* blue. My mistake."

"Look—" Susan tried not to grit her teeth "—don't go reading anything into the fact that I know what color Kyle Gordon's eyes are."

"Oh, I'd never—"

"I mean, I know what color that grotesque gas-guzzling car he careens around in—without benefit of a seat belt, I might add—is, too. But that does *not* imply I'm attracted to it in any way, shape or form. I wouldn't accept an engraved invitation to get into that thing!"

"Too bad," came the lightning-quick riposte. "Because if even a quarter of the stories I've heard about Kyle and that car are true, you could be missing one of the best back-seat rides in history."

"*Ramona!*"

The other woman gestured. "Sorry," she apologized, then lapsed into silence.

After a moment, Susan bent her head and went back to her paperwork.

There was a long pause. Finally Ramona spoke.

"You know," she began reflectively, "it's got to be awfully hard on him."

Susan set down her pen. Enough, she decided. "Ramona—"

Her friend went on speaking. "I mean, when I think back... Did Mike ever tell you that Kyle's father was a combat pilot for the U.S. Air Force? Flew in Vietnam? Was decorated three or four times?"

"Yes," Susan answered tersely. "He also told me how Kyle ended up being adopted by H. G. Gordon after his parents were killed in a car crash when he was six. But I really don't—"

Ramona interrupted, picking up the thread of her previous comments. "He probably heard about flying from the time he was a baby. Heaven knows, he was already hooked on planes when I met him in second grade. I remember that's all he'd draw in art classes. It used to make the teacher nuts. Still, even if he hadn't had his eye on the sky before he came to Wilder's Forge, you can just bet his uncle would have turned him on to the wild blue yonder. Of course, a lot of guys daydream about flying. But Kyle followed through. Graduated from the Air Force Academy with honors. Became a pilot. Got picked for the space program."

Susan nodded once, her throat tight. Kyle's selection for the space program had come shortly after Mike's death. His achievement had made headlines in the local paper. There'd even been talk of holding some kind of ceremony to honor the high-flying hometown boy.

"And then—" Ramona snapped her fingers and shook her head "—it was all over. A training accident caused by somebody else's carelessness ruptured something in his ear and he was out. And not just out of the space program, either. Out of the Air Force, too. He was permanently grounded. No more flying—ever." She sighed. "Like I said, it's got to be awfully hard."

"I suppose," Susan conceded slowly. "Even so, the way Kyle—" She broke off with a gasp of dismay as she glanced at her wristwatch. "Oh, no. It's four-fifteen, Ramona. I've got to get out of here and pick up Charlie."

"Four-fifteen?" Ramona repeated, her eyes widening. "Lord, I'm due at a meeting about graduation in the principal's office." She got off Susan's desk. She started to turn away, then checked herself and said sincerely, "Look, Susan, I didn't mean to get you stirred up about Kyle."

"It's okay, Ramona."

"And about that little trick I pulled about the color of Kyle's—"

"It's *okay,* Ramona."

The brunette studied Susan silently for a few seconds. "Okay," she echoed finally. "I'll see you tomorrow."

"Tomorrow," Susan concurred, swiftly tidying her desk.

Ramona got all the way to the door of the classroom, then pivoted. "Susan?"

"Mmm?"

"I meant what I said before. About life going on. Mike wouldn't want you calling it quits because he's gone. He would have wanted you to be—" she gestured "—fulfilled."

Susan looked at her friend. She knew Ramona had her best interests at heart. She also knew the words Ramona had just spoken were true. Mike had been very clear about his hopes for her future during his final weeks.

"I haven't called it quits, Ramona," she defended herself. "And I'm perfectly fulfilled."

"Have you seen a man—socially—since Mike died?"

Susan flashed back on the scene at Fiori's Pizza Palace. "If seeing men socially is the key to a woman's fulfillment, then Wendy Marino must be the most fulfilled female in the world."

Ramona's brows went up. "Bitchy, bitchy."

"But accurate."

"True." Ramona regarded Susan shrewdly. "You know, it seems to me Jack said something about seeing Wendy wiggling around Fiori's, too. That wouldn't have anything to do with your—"

"No."

"Uh-huh. Let's go back to my original question, shall we? Have you seen a man socially since Mike died?"

Susan sighed. "No," she replied. There was no point in lying about her situation. She knew that Ramona, like most of the people in Wilder's Forge, was well aware of the facts.

"Do you want to? Start dating again?"

Susan hesitated. She had the distinct feeling she was being manipulated. She just hoped the manipulations had nothing to do with Kyle Gordon. The possibility that they did was certainly there. Ramona obviously liked the man. She'd also made it clear that she thought Susan needed to get out and about more.

"That would depend on whom the date was going to be with, Ramona," she answered carefully, getting up from her chair.

"How about Jack?"

The inquiry caught Susan completely off guard. She gaped for a second before finding her voice. "Your *brother?*"

A nod of confirmation.

"I, but, Ramona, don't be silly. Jack's not interested in me!"

Ramona smiled. "Oh, really? Then why was he so insistent I find out whether you've got something going with Kyle Gordon?"

Kyle glanced at his wristwatch two days later as he jogged up to the front of his uncle's house.

Ten miles in an hour and ten minutes, he told himself. Not bad, all things considered.

It would've been better if you hadn't dogged that stretch by the high school, the voice inside his skull observed. *What were you hoping? That Susan would look out the window of her classroom and see you?*

I don't—Kyle stretched, extending his arms above his head in a slow, seamless movement—even know which classroom— he stretched again—is hers.

Oh, don't you? After all those questions you asked H.G. the other night at dinner about the times he talked to her classes, you weren't able to figure out which room is hers?

Look, I'm not responsible for the fact that her classroom happens to be on the side of the high school the road runs by!

No, but you did—

Shut up for a minute and let me check my pulse.

The voice did.

Kyle pressed the tips of his fingers against the pulse point in his neck. Keeping an eye on the sweep hand of his watch, he counted.

A little fast, he conceded when he was finished.

Thinking about Susan Brooks has always had that effect on you, hasn't it? the voice piped up.

It's the damned medication I'm taking, Kyle countered.

Yeah, right. Lie to yourself, hot dog. But don't lie to me. I know better.

You don't know anything I don't.

I know you're going to cramp up with more knots than a box of pretzels if you don't do a few more stretches.

The voice had a point. And having made it so pointedly, it subsided into silence.

Kyle finished cooling down, then opened the front door of his uncle's house and went in. "H.G.?" he called, stripping off the T-shirt he'd been wearing and drying his sweat-sheened chest and arms with it.

"In my office!"

Kyle found his uncle pretty much as he'd left him when he'd gone out for his run. "Still going through boxes, hmm?" he asked, watching the older man finish slicing through the sealing tape on a particularly large and battered-looking carton.

"I brought a few more down from the attic."

"I see. Are you any closer to finishing the new book?"

H.G. shrugged. "It's all up in my head," he replied. "It's just not ready to come out yet. But as soon as it is . . ."

"You'll be at the word processor day and night."

"That's how it usually works."

Kyle nodded, well aware that H.G.'s seemingly lackadaisical attitude about his writing tended to give way to a literary frenzy as his deadlines drew near. "Find anything interesting in the cartons?" he inquired.

"As a matter of fact . . ." The older man paused, sat back on his heels and glanced around. "Now where did I . . . Aha!" He reached to his right, picked something up off the floor and brandished it triumphantly. "Remember this?"

The "this" in question was made out of metal and looked a lot like a handgun. Kyle needed a moment to recognize it for what it was.

"My BB pistol!" he exclaimed.

"It won't fire," H.G. remarked. "I tried."

Kyle chuckled. "I think it was pretty much ruined the night Mike and I camped out in the woods and nearly drowned in a thunderstorm. We were in such a hurry to get in out of the rain we left it and a bunch of other stuff at our campsite." He chuckled a second time. "I can't believe you kept that thing all these years."

The older man set down the gun and turned his attention to the contents of the box he'd finished opening a few moments earlier.

"Actually," he replied, rummaging around with great enthusiasm, "it's been my experience that you don't realize how much something means to you until after you've gotten rid of it. That's one reason I've been glad to let you keep your T-bird here all these years. I knew that someday... Hello, hello, hello! What in heaven's name is this?"

Kyle watched as his uncle extracted a round object about the size of a cantaloupe from the carton. The ball-shaped thing was made out of a silvery-toned metal. It had an odd oil-on-water sheen.

Kyle took a step forward, his gaze fixed on the item H.G. was holding. "It's the Orb," he breathed, assailed by a rush of boyhood memories.

H.G. looked up. He was smiling. "I beg your pardon?"

"The Orb," Kyle repeated, still staring at the sphere. "I found it in the woods at the edge of Cumming's Meadow the summer you were up against a deadline for that time-travel trilogy you did."

"The summer Mike Brooks's family moved to Wilder's Forge?"

"That's right. But I found it before I met him. I remember, I was out exploring..."

"By yourself?"

Kyle shrugged. "There wasn't anyone in Wilder's Forge I wanted to hang out with before Mike showed up."

Still smiling, H.G. stroked the surface of the silver ball. Kyle found that he itched to do the same. "What did you call this? The...Orb?"

"Yeah. I think I learned the word from one of your books. I remember you making me look it up when I asked you what it meant."

"It's a very fitting name." H.G. continued stroking the ball. "Strange, though. I don't recall having seen this particular object before."

"Like I said, you were crashing on a book when I found it."

"In other words, you could have dropped this, ah, Orb on my head and I wouldn't have noticed," the older man translated. "But afterward. After I finished the book. Did you show it to me then?"

"I don't think so. I'd probably lost interest and stuck it away in my closet or something by that time, H.G. My attention span was pretty short when I was a kid. There was always something new and exciting coming over the horizon." Kyle held out his hands, palms up. "Do you mind?"

"Do I . . . ? Oh. No. Of course not."

H.G. lobbed the silvery globe to Kyle in a gentle arc. Kyle caught it easily.

He'd forgotten how light the thing was. How . . . good it felt to hold. It was sleek but not slippery and it seemed to warm at his touch. Kyle briefly entertained the fanciful notion that this unusual souvenir from his childhood was reacquainting itself with him in the same way he was reacquainting himself with it.

He drew random geometric patterns on the sphere with his fingertips. The metallic surface was absolutely smooth. Utterly flawless. He smiled suddenly, recalling that he'd once taken a hammer to the Orb in an unsuccessful bid to find out whether it was hollow.

Subtlety never has been your strong suit, has it? the voice inside his skull inquired in an unusually benign tone.

No, Kyle frankly admitted. I've always favored the direct approach.

Except with Susan.

Yeah, well, she seems to be the exception to a lot of . . .

The realization that H.G. was speaking to him brought Kyle out of his reverie. "Ah, what did you say?" he asked.

"I said, there was another series of sightings last night. To the west. Near Peekskill."

Kyle had no need to inquire what kind of sightings his uncle was talking about. As a science fiction writer, H. G. Gordon had always had an interest in the UFO phenomenon. That interest had intensified over the years, fueled in part by the fact that New York's Hudson Valley—where Wilder's Forge was located—seemed to be a magnet for UFO incidents.

"Oh?"

"It's the third cluster in six weeks. There's a lot of commonality this time. You know, majority agreement on the size and shape of the object, the color and configuration of the lights. Plus, there's virtual unanimity on the observation that whatever it was moved very slowly, went into a hovering mode and made little or no sound. I got a couple of phone calls about it while you were—" He stopped abruptly.

"H.G.?" Kyle prompted. His feelings about the whole UFO question were mixed. Although he agreed with those who contended it was the height of arrogance to assume that humans were the only sentient beings in the universe, he'd had a couple of unpleasant brushes with members of what he privately labeled the "close encounters crowd" during his Air Force service.

"I just remembered," his uncle said. "There was a call for you. A woman."

Kyle's breath wedged at the top of his throat. He nearly dropped the Orb. *Susan,* he thought instantly.

His whole body seemed to suffuse with warmth.

"Did she leave a name?" he asked after a moment.

H.G. nodded and gestured vaguely toward his desk. "I took a message. She said she knew you from California."

Kyle's hopes nosedived. He tightened his grip on the Orb.

"I see," he said quietly. Picking a careful path around the obstacle course of cartons, he made his way to his uncle's paper-strewn desk. He set down the silvery sphere very gently and started going through the clutter.

You didn't really think Susan Brooks called you, did you? the voice needled with renewed nastiness.

I don't know what I thought, Kyle retorted.

You were right on the money the other day, hot dog. She doesn't like you very much. As a matter of fact, she's never liked you very much. Not even when you were one hundred percent fit and flying. And now that you're nothing but a—

"That's it," H.G. said. "That green slip of paper."

Kyle looked at the specified slip. It took him several seconds to decipher his uncle's atrocious handwriting.

"Jenna Bradley," the scrawled message stated. "May be in neighborhood next month."

The image of a shapely redhead with sparkling green eyes formed in Kyle's mind.

"Girlfriend of yours?" his uncle queried.

Kyle wasn't certain how to answer that question. But even if he had been, he wouldn't have had a chance. H.G. kept right on talking.

"She didn't seem too bright," the older man remarked.

Kyle was stung by the apparent link between this comment and the assumption implied by the previous inquiry. While he was willing to admit that he tended to favor beauty over brains when it came to his romantic involvements, he'd never gone in for the dazzling but hopelessly dim types.

Well, maybe not never, he conceded. But not for a long time. Jenna was a case in point. Her intellectual attributes were at least as impressive as her physical endowments.

Oh, right, the voice inside his skull drawled sarcastically. *You picked Jenna up at that NASA party because you admired her IQ.*

"Gee, thanks, H.G.," Kyle said with an edge. "A woman calls, she doesn't seem too bright, so you assume she must be a girlfriend."

The older man looked distressed. "Oh, no. No, Kyle," he protested. "I didn't assume... Well, yes, I suppose I did. But I wasn't being critical of her. I'm sure this—what's her name again? Janet? Jennie?"

"Jenna."

"Yes. Of course. I'm sure this Jenna is a lovely person. I simply meant she didn't strike me as being any, ah, rocket scientist."

Kyle's mouth twisted at his uncle's choice of words. "Actually, she's got a Ph.D. in radio astronomy."

H.G.'s brows soared skyward. "Well, I wish I'd realized!" he responded, plainly chagrined. "What's her position on SETI?"

Kyle started shuffling through the fistful of notes and message slips he was still holding. "To tell you the truth, we never discussed the Search for Extraterrestrial Intelligence."

"But you *do* support—"

"Sure, H.G. Sure. You know I do. I have a lot of respect for most of the people involved in the SETI effort. Of course, I could do without the folks who claim the Air Force has a bunch of charred alien corpses from a crashed flying saucer squirreled away in a hangar in—" He broke off in midsentence as his gaze suddenly locked onto the name written on the bottom of a scrap of paper he was about to discard—A. Pettit.

Later—much, much later—Kyle realized that the name probably wouldn't have registered if he and his uncle had been talking about something other than SETI.

"Kyle?"

He looked across the room at his uncle. "Do you know a man named Pettit?" he asked. "Alvin Pettit?"

"Why, yes," H.G. replied. "He phoned me about, oh, a month or so ago. It was shortly before you came home. He said we'd been introduced at a science fiction convention in Boston a few years back."

"He *said?* You didn't remember him?"

"No. But that's not unusual. I hardly ever remember people after the first introduction."

"What did he want?"

"He told me he was associated with NASA's SETI program. Naturally I was intrigued. Then he said he happened to be in the area and inquired if he might stop by to get my input on the Hudson Valley UFO sightings. He also expressed an interest in my listening project. Do you know, he was even aware that I'm using—"

"He came here?" Kyle cut in swiftly.

H.G. looked a trifle nettled at the interruption, but responded with a nod. "He stayed for about ninety minutes. He had identification. He insisted on flashing it as soon as I opened the door."

"All the two of you did was talk?"

A second nod. "What do you know about this Dr. Pettit, Kyle?"

"I know *of* him," Kyle answered, recognizing the distinct possibility that he was making a big deal about nothing. Seeing Pettit's name had startled him. "He has a reputation for being strange."

"Oh, really?"

"He didn't seem that way to you?"

"Not particularly," H.G. replied. The corners of his mouth twitched suddenly and a mischievous twinkle appeared in his eyes. "Of course, my tolerance for strangeness is probably substantially higher than most people's. Now I'm not saying I'd like to count Dr. Pettit among my most intimate friends— someone really should give him a hint about his dandruff and bad breath, you know. Nonetheless, he didn't appear to me to be outside the parameters of acceptable peculiarity."

Kyle decided it was pointless to pursue the subject any further. Whether Alvin Pettit was, indeed, the obnoxious, ill-kempt oddball gossip proclaimed him to be didn't really matter. The man had come and gone and apparently done no harm.

Kyle dropped the scrap of paper with Alvin's name on it back into the disorder on top of his uncle's desk.

"I'm going to go and take a shower, H.G.," he said. "Forget I said anything about Alvin Pettit, okay? Well, no. Don't forget it completely. If he contacts you again, I'd like to know."

"Of course," his uncle agreed.

Kyle headed for the door.

"Kyle?"

Kyle stopped and turned. "Yeah?"

"Don't you want your Orb?"

Three

_____

"My mom wants to talk to you," Charlie announced to Kyle five days later. He held out the telephone he'd had pressed to his ear.

Kyle accepted the proffered receiver with a peculiar sense of edginess. The way he felt reminded him of descriptions he'd read about the butterflies-in-the-stomach anxiety teenage boys supposedly suffer when they first begin asking girls out for dates. Such social uncertainty had been alien to him during adolescence. It wasn't alien to him now.

"Thanks, Charlie," he said, lifting the telephone to his own ear. He inhaled deeply, like a diver preparing for a plunge.

Susan beat him to the jump. "Kyle?"

His mouth went dry. His palms grew damp. Man, there was something about hearing _her_ voice saying _his_ name that really got to him.

Kyle cleared his throat and shifted his weight. "Yeah," he affirmed, rubbing his free hand against his jean-clad thigh. "Is there a problem?"

"I hope not. Look, I want you to know I appreciate all the attention you've been giving Charlie...."

"Hey, he's one terrific kid."

"Well, yes. I certainly think so. But I don't want you to feel you've got some kind of obligation to him."

"Obligation?"

"Because of Mike."

"Susan—"

She overrode him. "I know Charlie is a bit of a con artist. He'd love to wheedle his way into spending most of the summer with you."

"Would that be so bad?"

There was a short silence on the other end.

God, Kyle thought, stung. Maybe she thinks it would be! Maybe she thinks I'm some sort of negative influence on Charlie.

The possibility that Susan could have such an opinion rankled him.

"I don't want him taking advantage of you," she finally said.

"Don't worry," Kyle retorted tersely. "He won't."

No kidding, the ubiquitous voice concurred. *Nobody ever takes advantage of you, do they, hot dog? You're always one step ahead of the game. The moving target. And when it comes to con artists—*

Shut up! Kyle snarled silently. He was getting sick and tired of having his life picked apart by this snottily superior mental commentator. Okay. So he liked having his own way. Who didn't? And maybe he wasn't above using a little psychology to get what he wanted. Big deal! He wasn't perfect. He'd never claimed to be. He was well aware that he had his share of flaws. But he'd learned to live with them.

Maybe you should have learned to fix them, the voice suggested, firing off one last shot before retreating into silence.

"Fine. I won't worry," Susan replied, a hint of starch in her tone. "But about this lunch today—"

"My idea," Kyle interrupted flatly. "My invitation. It's a simple yes or no situation. Your call."

He'd encountered Charlie about twenty minutes earlier. He'd been driving to the supermarket for his uncle. The kid had been

biking along the road alone. He'd slowed down and pulled
over. Charlie had pedaled up and stopped beside the car, plainly
pleased to see him.

One thing had quickly led to another. Kyle had soon suggested that Charlie stow his bike in the trunk of the car and join
him for lunch. A celebration of the start of summer vacation,
he'd said.

*Another chance to tell stories about your gone-forever glory
days to an uncritical audience,* the voice had amended.

Charlie had snapped at the idea of lunch like a trout going
after a fly. But he'd stopped short of accepting Kyle's invitation. Doing that, he'd reluctantly admitted, was contingent on
obtaining his mother's permission.

"She acts like I'm a baby, Kyle," he'd groused. "It isn't like
I can't take care of myself. Jeez! I'm going to be in sixth grade
next year."

Kyle's first impulse had been to support the boy's obvious
desire to loosen the apron strings. He'd opened his mouth,
ready to express the opinion that it really wouldn't be that awful if Charlie went off and did what he wanted to without receiving Mom's official okay.

Something had kept him from uttering the words. He didn't
know what it had been. Certainly not the damned voice inside
his head. He only knew that rather than encouraging Charlie
to rebel against Susan's rules as he'd intended, he'd ended up
reinforcing them.

"Your mom will figure out how grown-up you are eventually, Charlie," he'd heard himself promise. He'd sounded dis-
concertingly avuncular. Almost . . . paternal. Which was pretty
absurd, considering that he was no more prepared to take on
the responsibilities of being a father than he was to accept the
restrictions of being a husband. "In the meantime, let's go find
a pay phone so you can give her a call."

The sound of Susan sighing came over the line. "Well, if
you're certain you don't mind—"

"I'm positive."

"All right, then," she capitulated. "Would you please put
my son back on?"

"Sure." Kyle wondered fleetingly whether Susan had meant to inflect the words "my son" as oddly as it seemed to him she had. He handed the phone back to Charlie, giving the kid a quick thumbs-up signal as he did so. The kid beamed in response and put the receiver to his ear.

"Yeah?" he said into the mouthpiece. He paused, listening expressionlessly. "Yeah. Okay. Huh? But that's not..." He paused again, rolling his eyes this time. Then, grumpily, "Okay. Huh? No. Of course not. For Pete's sake, how can I be taking Kyle's valuable time, Mom? He doesn't have anything to do. He doesn't even have a job right now! What? Yeah. Yeah. Be home by three or I lose my TV privileges until the next century. 'Bye, Mom."

And with that, Charlie hung up.

"Jeez..." he muttered, packing a wealth of preadolescent exasperation into the single syllable.

Normally, Kyle would have responded with a wisecrack or some show of guy-to-guy solidarity. But something he'd heard Charlie tell Susan had left him too raw to do either.

"How can I be taking up Kyle's valuable time, Mom?" the kid had wanted to know. "He doesn't have anything to do. He doesn't even have a job right now!"

Kyle looked up at the midday June sky. It was so crystalline clear. So blazingly blue. So full of promises and possibilities.

How many times in the past had he stared up at such a clear blue sky and known he could claim those promises and possibilities for his own? he asked himself. How...many...times?

He closed his eyes for a moment, sucking in a short, sharp breath through his nose. A sense of loss sliced into him like a stiletto blade.

Kyle understood that Charlie hadn't been passing judgment on him when he'd said what he'd said to Susan. But there was no getting around the fact that it had sounded like a condemnation. He also knew the kid hadn't intended any harm with his words. Still, that hadn't prevented them from hurting.

"Kyle?" Charlie asked.

Kyle opened his eyes. Schooling his features, he forced himself to bring his gaze back to the ground. "Yeah?"

"Are you okay? You look sort of...weird."

Kyle instinctively turned on a variation of the Gordon Grin. It felt a lot like the smile he'd managed to manufacture after the accident that had ended his career. Within seconds of regaining consciousness, he'd realized that something was seriously, maybe irreparably, wrong with him. He, the fearless fighter pilot, had been terrified. Hence the smile. He would have died rather than let anyone know how scared he was.

"Your eyes must be playing tricks on you, buddy," he responded, rumpling Charlie's hair. "There's nothing wrong with me that a big lunch won't fix." It was a lie, but he made it sound like the gospel truth. "So, what do you want to eat? Greasy burgers and fries slathered with catsup? No. Wait. *I* know. What you're really craving is a nutritious serving of low-fat yogurt and a vitamin-packed salad, right?"

Charlie faked the sound of retching.

"You don't like the idea of rabbit food, huh?"

"No way!" the kid declared. "Can we go to Fiori's again?"

"We can go anywhere you want, Charlie."

Susan contemplated several courses of action once she hung up after her conversation with Charlie and Kyle. The most constructive of the lot involved banging her head against the refrigerator door to try to knock a little sense into herself.

She'd handled the telephone episode badly and she knew it. But she hadn't been able to stop herself. The moment Charlie had gotten on the line and uttered the name Kyle as though it held the secrets of the universe, her hackles had gone up.

She knew part of her response stemmed from jealousy. Somehow, some way, in the course of less than a month, Kyle Gordon had established a bond with her son that was totally independent of her. As galling as it was for her to admit, he gave Charlie something she couldn't.

But how long would he go on giving it? That question nagged at Susan every time she contemplated Kyle's relationship with Charlie. That question was another reason for her hostile response to the sound of his name.

What if, after all his protestations about what a terrific kid Charlie was, Kyle got bored with youthful hero worship and sought a more adult source of attention? What would happen to her son then?

Charlie had already lost his father. Mike's untimely death had hurt him terribly. While he'd recovered from the pain with remarkable resilience, Susan didn't know whether he'd be able to cope with another loss.

She closed her eyes and clenched her hands into fists. Damn Kyle Gordon! she thought angrily. Did he have any idea how he affected people? Did he ever consider how easily he could disrupt their lives with his charm and his charisma and his killer grin? And if he did, did he care?

She made an inarticulate sound of frustration.

Despite her repeated efforts to shove him out of her mind, she was still thinking about Kyle Lochner Gordon far too much. And not just in connection with her concerns about Charlie, either.

What was worse, she'd actually started *dreaming* about him! Just the other night, he'd invaded her slumbers in the guise of a futuristic superhero. He'd ascended from a cloudless sky clad in nothing but a crash helmet, aviator-style sunglasses, a midnight blue velvet cape and a skintight pair of bikini briefs.

The briefs had appeared to be made out of aluminum foil. They'd also been emblazoned with what looked like a bolt of lightning.

He'd told her he was there to save her. From whom or what he hadn't made clear. It hadn't seemed to matter. She'd been too busy speculating about the significance of the lightning bolt to pursue the issue.

Their eyes had met and locked. She'd felt her lips part. Her heart had started performing Olympic-style tumbling tricks.

Kyle the Superhero had held out his right hand to her. "Come fly with me," he'd invited.

It had been an incredibly corny line. Even fast asleep, some portion of her brain had recognized this and demanded an immediate rewrite. But the *way* that line had been spoken . . .

Susan hadn't been able to resist.

Slowly, ever so slowly, she'd reached out to clasp Kyle's hand. She'd known this was a life-altering moment, and she hadn't wanted to rush through it or get it wrong. She'd opened her mouth to speak, to tell him how much she—

Brrrrng.

Susan started violently.

Brrrrng.

It was the telephone.

Struggling to compose herself, Susan picked up the receiver. "H-hello?" she said.

"Hello, Susan?"

The voice was male. A poised and pleasant baritone. Although Susan knew she'd heard it before, she couldn't link it to a name or face.

"Ah . . . yes," she said after a moment.

"This is Jack Wiley."

Susan caught her breath.

"Jack!" she exclaimed, cringing inwardly at the artificial brightness in her tone. "Hello. I didn't recognize your voice. How are you?"

"Fine. Just fine. I—I haven't caught you at a bad time, have I? You seem a bit, ah—"

Susan cut in before her caller could complete his description. "No, this isn't a bad time. I was just standing around, uh, thinking."

She was profoundly grateful that Jack didn't inquire into the nature of her thoughts. There might come a time when she'd be willing to share a description of Kyle the Lightning-Bolted Superhero with her close friend, Ramona. But with Ramona's brother? With the principal of Charlie's school? No. She didn't think so.

"Good. Good," came his agreeable response. "I hope your summer vacation is off to a pleasant start."

"Very pleasant. And yours?"

"I've still got a few items to take care of before I can officially close the books and shift into a relaxation mode."

There was a brief pause. Eventually Susan queried, "Is there something I can do for you, Jack?"

"Well, yes. That is, I hope so. Do you have plans for this Friday evening?"

Susan shifted her weight and fluffed at her hair. "Nothing definite. Charlie and I had talked about going to the carnival this weekend. You know the one in…" She mentioned a nearby town. "But that's about it."

"I see. In that case, perhaps you'd consider having dinner with me."

"On Friday?"

"Yes."

Susan hesitated, a complex series of emotions sleeting through her.

Given the conversation she'd had with Ramona a week before, she couldn't very well pretend that Jack's invitation had taken her by surprise. In point of fact, she'd been expecting him to call.

She'd even raised the possibility that she might start dating during a bedtime conversation with Charlie the night before. She hadn't mentioned any names, just gently tested the waters. With a few caveats, her son had been surprisingly amenable to the idea.

"I've been thinkin', Mom," he'd confided, smothering a yawn. "I'm ten now. In eight years—maybe even less if I get accelerated—I'll be going away to college. And then you'll be all by yourself. I'll have my own life—you know?"

Susan's heart had contracted painfully at her son's words. Charlie plainly had come to terms with one of the truths she'd been struggling against since Mike's death. He'd made peace with the idea that life goes on. Perhaps she should try to learn from him.

Jack Wiley was a nice man, Susan told herself. A mature, eligible and attractive man. He was a man she could very easily learn to like.

Above all, Jack Wiley was not—repeat, *not*—Kyle Gordon.

"Susan?"

Susan released the breath she hadn't realized she'd been holding. "Dinner Friday evening sounds lovely, Jack," she said.

Kyle was in the middle of washing his beloved T-bird when Charlie came biking up the gravel-covered drive to H.G.'s house.

"Hey, kid!" he called, rising from a squat. While Charlie's arrival was unexpected, it was not unwelcome. "What's happening?"

Nothing good, to judge by the kid's uncharacteristically careless treatment of his bike. Instead of dismounting and setting the kickstand, Charlie brought the two-wheeler to a skidding stop, hopped off and let it crash to the ground. He then stomped over to Kyle.

"You're not going to believe this, Kyle," he declared furiously. "You are totally not going to believe this!"

Kyle wiped his wet hands on the ratty pair of khaki cutoffs he was wearing. "What aren't I going to believe?"

"My *mom* is going on a *date!*"

For a moment, Kyle's brain balked. It simply refused to make sense of the words just spoken. "What?" he finally managed to get out.

"My mom is going on a date," Charlie repeated. After dragging the back of one hand beneath his nose, he added the kicker. "With my *principal!*"

"Jack Wiley?" A number of the conversations he'd had with Charlie had, quite naturally, centered around school. The first time the kid had mentioned the name of his school principal, Kyle's memory had flashed up a face from twenty years ago. A couple of questions, and he'd nailed the connection. His "Jack" and Charlie's "Mr. Wiley" were the same person.

"Yeah."

"When did this happen?"

More to the point, *how* did it happen? Although Kyle took no pride in admitting it, he'd done some digging into Susan's social life during the past week or so. He'd come up empty. The scuttlebutt in Wilder's Forge was that Mike Brooks's widow had buried her heart along with her husband.

"Yesterday. Mom told me this morning at breakfast."

"Jack Wiley called your mother out of a clear blue sky, asked her for a date and she said yes?" Kyle questioned dubiously. That didn't sound like the Susan Brooks he knew—thought he knew. It didn't sound like the Jack Wiley he remembered from high school, either.

"I told you you wouldn't believe it!" Charlie's glasses had slipped down from the bridge of his nose. He shoved them back into place. "I didn't even believe it at first. I mean, my *mom* and my *principal?*" His voice rose. "My life is *wrecked* if anybody at school finds out about this!"

Kyle took a step forward, and put his hands on the boy's narrow shoulders. "Hey, take it easy, buddy," he advised. "It's not that bad."

"Yes, it is!" Charlie insisted, pulling away. "Maybe nobody will find out about *this* date. But what if they have more? And what if it's not just dates? What if they end up getting *married* or something?"

Kyle got a very hollow feeling in the pit of his stomach. It suddenly occurred to him that the Jack Wiley he remembered had had a lot of things in common with Mike Brooks. They'd both been presidents of the Wilder's Forge High School student council. Both of them had been voted Most Likely to Succeed by their respective classmates. And neither of them had ever shown up at a standardized test without an adequate supply of perfectly sharpened Number Two pencils.

Of course Mike had had a subversive streak. He'd been a rebel—although generally with a worthy cause—when the circumstances had required it. He'd also possessed a devilish sense of humor.

Jack Wiley, on the other hand, had always been toe-the-line, white-bread bland. He'd been the kind of guy who'd had to have jokes explained to him. Even the dirty ones.

Nonetheless . . .

"I think you're getting way ahead of yourself here," Kyle told Charlie. His throat and chest felt tight. His voice sounded the same way. An unfamiliar emotion was gnawing at his gut. "Millions of people go out on dates every day. Most of them don't end up getting married to each other."

"Yeah, but some of them do," Charlie countered, getting more and more upset. "They go out on dates and they decide they're in love and they get married. That's how it works!"

"Charlie—"

Like an overwound spring, the kid suddenly appeared to snap. "I *never* would have said it was okay for her to have dates if I thought it was going to be Mr. Wiley asking her, Kyle,'' he declared in a rush. "I thought it was going to be you!"

There was a pause. Charlie's shrill words seemed to hang, trembling, in the balmy air.

"You thought *I* was going to ask your mother out?'' Kyle finally said. He removed the sunglasses he was wearing and looked down at Charlie.

The boy nodded, then shifted nervously. Kyle had the impression Charlie was deeply embarrassed by his outburst.

"You said something about it to her?"

"Oh, no.'' Charlie flushed. "See, the other night before I went to bed, Mom and me had this talk. I told her some of the stuff you told me about Dad. You know. About those cool things you did when you were in high school? Like stealing that other team's mascot?"

Kyle experienced a twinge of anxiety. He'd played fast and loose with a few of the key facts when he'd regaled Charlie with tales of his and Mike's adolescent adventures. While he believed his reasons for doing so were good ones, he had a sneaking hunch Susan might not agree.

"Anyway," Charlie went on, "Mom got this strange look on her face. I think maybe she was surprised by the stuff you told me. Because, like, she only knew my dad when he was older. When he was all settled down. And he probably never told her about how he was a wild and crazy guy in high school. I mean, he must have figured she wouldn't understand.'' Charlie wrinkled his forehead, momentarily distracted from the matter at hand. "Have you ever noticed that girls don't understand a lot of things guys do?"

"More times than I'd care to count, kid,'' Kyle answered dryly. He'd noticed the reverse, as well, of course, but this wasn't the time to mention it. "Go on."

"Well, there was this pause. Mom still looked kind of strange. Like something was bothering her. After about a minute she said she wanted to ask me something important. So I said, 'What?' And she said, 'How would you feel if I went out on a date with somebody?' I was really surprised. I mean, she *never* asked me anything like that before. I told her I guessed

I'd feel okay about it. Unless the guy was a major ax murderer or something.''

"I . . . see.''

"Then I said some stuff about my going away to college. About how she'd be all by herself once I did.'' Charlie sighed heavily. "I don't think that would be very good for her.''

The pieces fell into place for Kyle. "You're worried about her.''

"I don't want her to be lonesome,'' the boy replied simply.

"And that's why you told her it'd be okay with you if she started going out on dates.''

"Yeah.'' Charlie looked down at his sneakered feet. "But like I said, I didn't think she was going to be doing it with Mr. Wiley.''

"You thought she was going to be doing it with . . . me.''

Kyle braced himself for a nasty crack from his inner voice. Surprisingly, it didn't come.

"Yeah.'' Charlie swallowed as much of the syllable as he spoke.

"Why would you think that, buddy?'' It was a dangerous question and Kyle knew it. He also knew he had no choice but to ask. If Charlie had picked up on his attraction to Susan, the attraction he'd been doing his best to keep under wraps, it was possible she'd sensed it, too.

God, Kyle thought, a chill running up his spine, maybe she'd sensed it from the very first. Maybe she'd had him pegged for the past eleven years, ever since the wedding.

Charlie lifted his head and met Kyle's gaze. "You asked me a lot of questions about her,'' he explained with a hint of defensiveness. "And you always seemed real interested when I said stuff about her. Plus, well, you know last week when you, me and Mom had lunch at Fiori's?''

"Yeah.''

"Well, I noticed you got this, uh, goony look in your eyes a couple of times.''

"*Goony?*''

"Uh-huh. Mom had it, too.''

His mind racing, Kyle searched his memory of what had happened at Fiori's nine days ago. As much as he would have liked to reject Charlie's "goony look" characterization, honesty forced him to admit that the kid was probably right on target—or close to it. Susan's presence at lunch had had an intoxicating effect on him. And while he knew his ability to disguise his feelings was very, very good, he was ruefully aware that it wasn't perfect.

But as for the matter of *her* having a goony look because of *him* . . .

No, Kyle told himself. It just didn't wash. He was no novice at reading women's responses to him. Granted, there were plenty of times when he found the opposite sex bewildering in the extreme. But there was no way he could be so far off the beam in his assessment of how Susan felt about him.

And yet . . .

Kyle suddenly thought about the way Susan had blushed when they'd met in the video-game arcade. He thought about the flashes of emotion he'd glimpsed streaking through the depths of her lovely brown eyes on that same occasion, too. None of those things spoke of indifference.

Was it possible? he wondered. Could Susan—

"Kyle?"

Kyle controlled a start of surprise. He was far less effective in controlling the abrupt acceleration of his pulse. "Yeah, Charlie?"

"Are you—" the kid swallowed "—mad at me?"

"About what? That you thought I might ask your mom out?"

"Yeah."

Kyle shook his head. "No. I'm not mad you."

"Good." Charlie chewed his lower lip for a moment. "You still could, you know," he ventured in a tentative tone. "Ask her out, I mean."

"Better me than your principal, huh?"

"Oh, *definitely.*"

Kyle felt one corner of his mouth kick up. So he still had a chance to ask Susan Brooks out, hmm? And with her son's heartfelt approval, no less.

It was something to contemplate.

"Charlie," he said slowly, "when is your mom's date with Mr. Wiley?"

"Friday." The youngster grimaced. "Oh. And listen to this. On top of everything, my mom wants me to have a *baby-sitter* when she goes out!"

Kyle might be more than two and a half decades Charlie's senior, but he could empathize with his indignation. "Insult to injury," he agreed.

"Yeah. Exactly."

Kyle considered the situation, then came to a decision. "I tell you what, buddy," he said, squaring his shoulders. "There's not a lot I can do about the principal. But I can damn well save you from the baby-sitter."

Four

By the time her Friday-night date with Jack Wiley came to a close and he pulled into the driveway of her house, Susan Brooks had concluded that she had a problem. She felt like a candidate for a self-help manual—something along the lines of "Supposedly Sane Women Who Are More Attracted to Stud Muffins than to Stable Men and How They Can Save Themselves Before It's Too Late."

The evidence of her problem was overwhelming. Consider:

She was at the end of her first social evening out in more than two years of widowhood. It had been an evening that could be summed up in a single one-syllable word. That word was "nice."

Her escort had been nice.

The restaurant he'd taken her to—in a solid seat-belt-equipped sedan that he drove at a responsible speed—had been nice.

The meal they'd eaten had been nice, too.

Ditto, the conversation they'd made during that meal.

Yet, despite this surfeit of niceness, all Susan wanted to do was say good-night to the man she was with and get rid of him. Because the sooner she did, the sooner she'd stop comparing him—unfairly and unfavorably—with Kyle Gordon.

"Here we are," Jack said pleasantly as he opened the door on Susan's side of the car.

"Thank you," she responded, allowing him to assist her out. She tried to ignore the twinge of distaste she experienced when she registered the softness of his hand.

Not for the first time that evening, Susan remembered the feel of Kyle's hand touching her own. The press of his labor-toughened palm. The clasp of his slightly callused fingers. She wondered what it would be like—

Stop it, she commanded herself. *Just stop it!*

"Did you say something?" Jack asked.

Susan blinked. Dear Lord, she certainly hoped not!

"Ah...no," she denied, patting at her hair. She'd worn it up that evening. Jack had complimented her on the style. Kyle hadn't seemed to notice it when he'd arrived to pick Charlie up for what he'd described as a "guys' night out."

As they walked to her front door, Susan tried to concentrate on her companion's strong points. So what if he had skinny lips and showed too much gum when he smiled? Big deal that his hair was growing thin and his waistline thick. Did it really matter that the thought of him wearing a velvet cape—much less lightning-emblazoned briefs—made her want to laugh? Jack Wiley was a *nice* man! He made her feel . . . comfortable.

What he didn't do was make her feel alive.

Only one man had done that since her husband's death.

They reached the front door. Susan opened her purse and searched for her keys.

"May I come in for a few minutes?"

Susan froze. She looked up from her purse. "In?"

Jack nodded.

"Oh, well, ah, I don't think that would be a very good idea, Jack." Susan glanced at her wristwatch. "You see, Charlie's going to be home soon and, well, it might be a little awkward."

"I see." Jack seemed content to accept her excuse. "You mentioned something earlier about his going to the carnival tonight. With Kyle Gordon?"

"That's right." She located her keys and extracted them from her purse.

"I gather you're, ah, friendly with Kyle?"

Susan felt herself flush. "Charlie certainly is," she answered. "And, of course, Kyle and Mike were very close."

"Of course."

There was a brief pause.

"Well, um, thank you for a lovely evening, Jack," Susan finally said.

"You're welcome," he returned. His gaze flicked downward. Susan swallowed. He was going to kiss her. She'd expected he might. She'd even made up her mind that if he went for her lips, she'd let him. She felt as though she owed him that, considering.

Jack went for her lips. But an instant before he claimed them, Susan turned her head. The movement was instinctive. Involuntary. The very opposite of what she'd planned. She wound up getting a clumsy peck on the cheek plus a quick whiff of minty-fresh male breath.

The scented breath irritated Susan. It seemed downright prissy. And she didn't much like the cologne Jack had on, either.

Jack stepped back. If her last-second rebuff had bothered him, he gave no sign of it. "Good night, Susan."

Susan forced a smile. "Good night, Jack."

Susan entered her house in an unsettled mood. Ninety minutes later she was pacing the carpeted floor of her living room, vacillating between anger and anxiety.

"Where *are* they?" she demanded of the empty room. "They were supposed to be home an hour ago!"

The possibility that something might have happened to Charlie weighed on her like a cold iron fist. Why had she let him go to the carnival with Kyle? she demanded of herself. She knew the way the man drove! He couldn't fly in the sky anymore, so he settled for speeding around the countryside in a car that only a testosterone-crazed teenage boy could love.

Stalking over to the living room's picture window, she drew back the curtains and peered out into the starlit night. Her heart leapt as she saw the headlights of a car coming around the curve in the road that ran by her house. It plunged a moment later when she realized the vehicle was not a Thunderbird convertible.

Her shoulders sagged. She let the curtain swing back into place and started pacing again.

She wondered if she should call the police. Surely they'd know if something had happened. If there'd been an accident at the carnival or a wreck on the road or...

She came to a halt in the middle of the living room. She closed her eyes, trying to stay calm. Any moment now, Kyle and Charlie would come tooling up the street, she told herself. They'd be safe and sound and they'd have an adequate explanation for putting her through this hell.

Her eyes popped open as an idea occurred to her. Kyle's uncle. Yes. *Yes!* She could call H. G. Gordon!

Pivoting, Susan headed toward the telephone in the kitchen. She was halfway there when she heard the rumble of a high-performance car engine.

She dashed back into the living room, arriving just in time to see a pair of headlights pierce through the picture-window curtains. A moment later, the beams went off. The sounds of two car doors being opened and closed followed.

"Thank God," Susan breathed. "Oh, thank God."

She crossed to the front door on wobbly legs. She flung it open. Half of her wanted to hug her son and hold him tight. The other half wanted to paddle his rear end with a hairbrush.

"Do you have any idea what time..." she began, then broke off as she focused on the two people standing before her.

Except for a sexy stubbling of new-beard growth and a smear of mustard on the front of the partially unbuttoned blue chambray shirt he was wearing, Kyle Gordon looked quite presentable. Her son looked anything but. Charlie's freckle-dusted face was pasty white, and his brown hair was standing up in tufts. The left leg of his jeans was ripped at the knee, and the red-and-white-striped T-shirt he had on was rumpled and stained.

He was toting a large teddy bear. The overstuffed creature was upholstered with fuchsia fur.

"Hi, M-Mom," Charlie quavered.

"Sorry we're a little late, Susan," Kyle said, deftly shepherding Charlie over the threshold.

That's when Susan smelled it. Or, to be more precise, that's when she smelled Charlie. Her nostrils quivered at the sour aroma emanating from her son.

"What happened?" she demanded, aghast.

Charlie produced a crooked grin, then glanced at Kyle. Stunned, Susan saw Kyle respond with what she could only describe as a conspiratorial wink. She watched with mounting outrage as her son met her gaze once again.

"One too many hot dogs, Mom," he explained. The crooked grin straightened slightly before he added unnecessarily, "I barfed."

"What do you mean you—"

"I'm okay now, though." Charlie thrust the teddy bear forward. "Here. Kyle and me won this for you at the carnival. Well, mostly Kyle won it. But I got to pick the prize. I hope you like it."

Susan had no choice but to accept the stuffed animal. It stared at her with blank, button-shaped eyes. "It's very... pink," she said.

"That lady who does your hair wanted Kyle to win one for her, too," Charlie commented. He burped.

It took Susan a second to figure out to whom her son must be referring. She turned to Kyle, glaring. "You were at the carnival with Wendy Marino?"

"No, Mom," her son responded. He burped a second time. "Kyle was at the carnival with *me*. We met up with Ms. Marino when we were getting cotton candy and sodas. She said Kyle should come to her salon so she could give him a blower job."

"She said *what?*" Susan's eyes slewed toward her son. She thought she heard Kyle start to chuckle, but when she cut her gaze to him, his lean-featured face was choirboy serious. She looked back at Charlie.

"A blower job," her ten-year-old repeated patiently. He clenched his right hand as though holding on to something, then gestured around his head. "She wants to fix up his hair with one of those hair-blower things."

There was a short, sharp silence.

"Oh," Susan finally said. She could feel Kyle watching her. She knew he was laughing inside.

"She didn't stay with us very long," Charlie concluded, rubbing his stomach. He wrinkled his brow. There was a con- strained quality to his voice when he resumed speaking. "I don't think she liked it much...when Kyle kissed the lady in the kissing booth...and the lady said...he could have an extra one for...free."

Susan glanced at Kyle. He gave her a roguish smile.

"I'm sure she didn't," she said through gritted teeth. "Look, young man. It's past your bedtime. I want you to—"

"Uh, 'scuse me, Mom. I gotta go to the bathroom."

Charlie made his exit with so little fuss that Susan didn't figure out exactly why he'd had to go to the bathroom until she heard him break into a run when he reached the hall. A mo- ment later, she heard a door slam.

She did what any mother would do. She dropped the fuzzy fuchsia teddy bear and turned to go to her son's aid.

"Don't," Kyle said sharply, catching her by the arm.

Susan tried unsuccessfully to jerk free. "My son needs me," she hissed, shocked by the tremor of response his touch evoked. "How dare you!"

"There's nothing daring about it. And there's nothing wrong with Charlie that he can't take care of himself. Give him a few minutes and he'll be fine. In the meantime, let him have his dignity."

"His *dignity?*" Again, Susan attempted to break away. Again, she failed. "We're talking about a sick ten-year-old child!"

"To you, he's a sick ten-year-old child. But as far as Char- lie's concerned, he's a guy who wolfed one too many hot dogs and has to pay the price. The last thing he wants is to have his mother holding his head over the toilet."

"But—"

"For God's sake, Susan." A very male kind of impatience sparked in Kyle's sky-colored eyes. "Why do you think he said, 'I gotta go to the bathroom,' instead of, 'Mommy, I'm gonna be sick'?"

Susan stiffened as the truth of Kyle's words struck home. Charlie's not a little boy anymore, she thought with a pang. Whether I'm ready for it or not, my son is growing up.

Life goes on.

The grip on her upper arm eased. "Okay?" Kyle asked in a gentler tone than he'd used previously.

Susan nodded, not quite trusting herself to speak.

A moment later, Kyle let go of her completely and took a step back. "Charlie'll be all right, Susan," he said. "Trust me. Think of this as a rite of passage."

A wry laugh escaped her. "For my son or for me?"

Kyle's mouth curved upward. A dimple creased his right cheek. "For your son. This could be one of the highlights of his summer. When he goes back to school and his buddies ask him what he did during vacation, I'll guarantee he'll give them a heave-by-heave account of this evening's episode."

"Guys...brag...about throwing up?"

"Oh, all the time. But don't worry if you don't get it. You're not supposed to." The dimple deepened. "You're a girl."

Susan had to smile.

"That's it," Kyle approved, grinning back at her. His teeth showed white against his tanned skin. The blue of his eyes seemed to intensify.

It would have been very easy for her to succumb to his charm at that moment, and Susan knew it. Maybe she would have. Maybe she would have forgiven and forgotten the emotional wringer he'd put her through, if Kyle hadn't raised his right hand and run it through his hair. The gesture reminded her of Charlie's comments about Wendy Marino. It also called attention to the very expensive wristwatch Kyle was wearing.

Susan stopped smiling. "You were an hour late, you realize," she stated flatly, steeling herself against his virile appeal.

Kyle's grin faded by degrees. She could practically see him calculating how to handle her sudden shift of mood.

"Yeah," he acknowledged after a moment. "I'm sorry."

"Did it occur to you that I might worry?"

"Hey, look." He gestured. "Charlie was with *me*, Susan."

The emphasis he put on the pronoun, the above-the-rules arrogance it seemed to imply, made Susan's temper flare. "Oh, that was supposed to relieve me of all anxiety?"

Kyle's features tightened. His posture went ramrod stiff. "Well, yeah," he responded. "I would've hoped you'd find it somewhat reassuring."

"Reassuring?" Susan flung the word back at him like a gauntlet. "Do you honestly see yourself as *reassuring?*"

His eyes went very dark. "Are you trying to tell me you think I'd let something bad happen to Charlie?"

Although he made no effort to close the distance between them, Susan's awareness of his physical proximity and power increased dramatically. Still, she didn't back off—or down. "Not intentionally," she answered.

"Meaning what?"

"Meaning—" she lifted her chin a notch "—you're careless."

Kyle stayed silent for nearly thirty seconds, his expression uncharacteristically introverted. Finally he drew a shuddery breath. His gaze refocused on Susan's face.

"Susan, I care about Charlie," he said. "I care about him because he's a great kid and because he's the son of one of the best men I ever knew. I would never do anything to hurt him. The fact that I forgot to watch the clock as closely as I should have tonight doesn't change that. I'm sorry we were late. I'm sorry you were upset. Now, what the hell else do you want me to say?"

His anger didn't surprise Susan. She didn't think Kyle was accustomed to have his personal code of conduct challenged. His confidence and charisma probably made it very simple for him to go his own way in life. Little wonder he'd found her characterization so unpalatable.

What did catch her off guard was her sense that he'd been hurt, truly hurt, by what she'd said. She'd had the impression it would take a harpoon to pierce Kyle's emotional hide. She'd assumed being called "careless" would be little more than a pinprick to him.

"Nothing," she answered, relenting. She'd made her point, she decided. There was no need to keep pounding it. "I don't want you to say anything else, Kyle. Except . . ."

"Except?"

"Except that you'll watch the clock a little more closely next time."

Susan saw the rigidity in Kyle's leanly muscular body ease by increments. The barest hint of a smile danced around the corners of his mouth, then disappeared. She wondered uneasily if she'd just been manipulated into perceiving vulnerability where none existed.

"You've got it."

There was a pause. Susan cocked an ear, listening for some indications of her son's condition. She thought she heard the sound of running water. Turning away from Kyle, she raised her voice and called, "Charlie? Are you all right?"

"Be out in a minute, Mom!" came the muffled response.

"See?" Kyle asked softly. "The kid's going to be fine."

Susan turned back to confront him. It seemed to her that the distance between them had shrunk during the past few seconds. She caught the faint tang of male sweat, unmasked by after-shave or cologne.

"Apparently so," she said. Her gaze slid downward from his face for a moment. Lord. Was it really necessary for him to have his shirt unbuttoned halfway to his navel? she asked herself.

"How was your date with Jack Wiley?"

Susan swallowed her first impulse, which was to answer with the word *nice*. "That's none of your business," she said.

"Is that what you're going to tell Charlie if he asks?"

"Why should Charlie—"

"You *do* realize that he isn't real enthusiastic about your going out with his principal, don't you?"

"I . . ." Susan was floundering. Although her son hadn't applauded the news that she'd accepted a date with Jack Wiley, he hadn't indicated any great objections, either.

"I think his exact phrase was, 'My life is wrecked if anybody at school finds out.'"

Brown eyes locked with blue. "You talked to Charlie about this?"

"*He* talked to *me.*"

Susan blinked. If Kyle was trying to get a bit of his own back because of her earlier criticism of him, he was doing a very good job. "I don't think—"

She broke off, her breath seeming to wedge in her throat as she saw Kyle's expression change. While the precise nature of this change was impossible to verbalize, its meaning was unmistakable.

A moment later he reached out and touched her hair. As light as it was, Susan felt the brushing contact clear down to her toes. Her stomach tightened. So did her nipples.

No, she thought. This isn't right. This shouldn't be happening.

"Let's not argue about Jack Wiley," Kyle said huskily. "There are much better things we can do."

He traced the outer curve of her right ear with his fingertips. Susan's pulse scrambled. "Stop that."

"Why?"

"Because—" she had to struggle to catch her breath "—you're making me uncomfortable."

Kyle's lips curved with devastating effect. A wicked gleam appeared in the depths of his eyes. "Is that uncomfortable bad or uncomfortable good?"

The question had a familiar ring. It took Susan a few seconds to remember where—and from whom—she'd previously heard it.

"Have you been talking to Ramona Bozeman?" she asked.

The gleam in Kyle's eyes got brighter. "Should I have been?"

"No!" The word came out a lot more emphatically than Susan intended it to. "I mean—"

"Have you and Jack Wiley's sister been discussing me behind my back, Susan?" Kyle's fingers had drifted from her ear to the curve of her cheek.

"Of . . . of course not," she lied, hating the breathless quality she heard in her voice. "W-why should I want to discuss you with . . . anyone?"

"Oh, I can think of lots of—"

"Hey, uh, Kyle?" Charlie suddenly called from the other end of the house. "Can you, uh, can you come here for a minute? Please? Now?"

Kyle's gaze didn't waver from Susan's face. "Sure thing, kid!" he called back.

Susan felt him stroke her cheek, then chart the shape of her lower lip with the pad of his thumb. She opened her mouth to say something. Kyle forestalled her with a shake of his head.

"Later," he said.

A moment after that, she was alone in her living room.

The events of that Friday night resonated in Susan's consciousness during the days that followed. And as they did, her resentment of Kyle Gordon grew. Deep down she knew she was more angry at herself than anyone else. But that didn't prevent her from directing her escalating sense of outrage at the man her son said he wanted to be "just like" when he got older.

Susan's emotions came to a head one week after her disturbing living-room encounter with Kyle. Not surprisingly, the catalyst for what happened was Charlie.

"I'm telling you the truth, Ramona," Susan said patiently, wedging the receiver of the kitchen telephone between her left ear and shoulder. She pulled the top off the carton of strawberry yogurt she'd just taken out of the refrigerator. "The evening was fine. We had a lovely time. Jack is a...very nice man."

"But you don't want to go out with him again," her friend said.

Susan smothered a sigh and stared down at the fruit-flecked dairy product she intended to have for lunch. She'd gotten on the scale that morning and discovered she'd gained a few pounds. She had the kind of figure that could go from pleasantly curvy to unpleasantly plump very rapidly. Rather than let things get out of hand, she'd decided it was time to start counting calories and grams of fat.

"Not really, no," she told Ramona.

Ramona clicked her tongue. "I didn't think it was going work. I mean, you're right about Jack's being nice. But you need someone with a lot more juice."

"It's not a question of—"

SLAM!

It was the front door.

"Hold on a sec, Ramona," Susan said. She covered the telephone mouthpiece. Her son had set off for a rendezvous with Kyle about ninety minutes before. She hadn't expected him back for hours. "Charlie?"

No answer. Just the stomp-stomp-stomp of her son going down the hall to his bedroom.

Another SLAM!

Susan's surprise turned to concern. She uncovered the mouthpiece. "Can I call you back?" she asked.

"Problem?"

"I'm not sure. Charlie just came in and he's slamming doors."

"Gotcha. 'Bye."

Susan hung up the phone, set down the carton of yogurt and headed to her son's room.

She knocked on the door. "Charlie?"

"Go away, Mom."

Susan paused. For better or worse, her attitude toward her son had been altered by some of the things Kyle had said to her the week before. Charlie was growing up. He deserved some privacy. Still...

"Is something wrong?" Susan asked.

"No!"

Susan paused again, every maternal instinct she possessed clamoring out an alarm. "Charlie. Please. I'd like to talk to you for a minute."

No answer. Susan waited nearly thirty seconds before deciding she'd been granted permission to enter. She opened her son's bedroom door slowly and peered in.

Charlie was sitting on his bed, staring fixedly into space. His back was rigid, his features stiff. He didn't acknowledge her intrusion.

"Hey, guy," Susan said softly.

She crossed to the bed and stood there for a few seconds, gazing anxiously down at her son. He looked . . . devastated. Now that she was close enough, she could see the dried track of a tear on his left cheek.

Anger sparked to life inside her. She sat down on the bed. "You want to tell me what's wrong?"

Charlie's mouth tightened. He shook his head.

"Maybe I can help."

Another shake of the head.

"Charlie . . ."

Her son turned toward her very suddenly. He was blinking rapidly, obviously trying not to cry. "It's K-Kyle."

Susan's spark of anger flared into a white-hot flame. "What about Kyle?"

Charlie swallowed. "We were gonna meet at the video arcade. He said he'd see me there today. So I went. Only . . . only he didn't show up."

"Oh, Charlie." She wanted to give him a hug. Something about his expression prompted her to opt for a comforting pat on the back, instead. "I'm sorry, honey. But, well, Kyle isn't the best person in the world when it comes to showing up when he says he'll show up."

Charlie sniffed. He knuckled his cheek. "I know that. So . . . so I waited pretty long. Then I started thinkin', like, maybe somethin' happened to him, you know? Maybe he crashed up his T-bird. Or maybe he had an accident at his uncle's house. His uncle isn't around right now. He had to go into New York City to talk to some big-deal scientist about this radio-frequency scanning he does. He thinks aliens are probably beaming messages at us, see, and he's trying to pick them up. But, anyway, Kyle's all by himself. So I got worried."

Susan's stomach knotted. She could see where this was leading. Damn! It was exactly what she'd been afraid of. She'd been afraid of it from the very start of Kyle's involvement with her son.

"You rode your bike over to H.G.'s house, didn't you, Charlie?" she asked quietly.

The boy nodded, his brows drawing together in a V. "I had to knock and knock before Kyle finally opened up the door.

H-he—'' his voice wobbled alarmingly ''—was really w-weird, Mom. Like, his eyes were all red and he hadn't shaved and his clothes looked like he'd been wearing them for a long time. Plus...he smelled kind of gross.''

He'd been drinking, Susan interpreted. He'd been boozing it up and he was hung over.

''At first he stared at me like he didn't even know who I was,'' her son went on. ''Then it was like he got mad that I was there. But before I could really say anything, I looked behind him and I saw this...this *lady*. She had on one of Kyle's shirts and she didn't seem very happy at all. I think she said something to Kyle and he maybe said something back. Then he looked at me again and...and...''

Susan gathered Charlie into her arms, wanting desperately to spare him what was plainly an anguished memory. ''Oh, sweetie, it's all right.''

''He told me to go away, M-Mom!'' Charlie choked out, burrowing his head against her shoulder. ''K-Kyle told me to go away and l-leave him alone!''

Susan drove to H. G. Gordon's house in a fury. She'd never been so angry in her life.

She didn't give a damn that Kyle Gordon had gotten drunk. She didn't give a damn that Mr. Stud Muffin with the killer grin had picked up some bimbo and taken her to bed, either. But when that selfish bastard did something to hurt her son...

She was glad Mike wasn't around to see this. She could only imagine how wounded he'd be by his best buddy's betrayal of his only son's trusting affection.

Slamming out of her car, she stalked up to H.G.'s front door. There was no excuse for what Kyle had done. Absolutely... positively...none.

She hammered on the door with her fist.

No answer.

She hammered a second time. She knew Kyle was inside. His car was in the driveway. So was a sporty silver import. The bimbo's mode of transportation, no doubt.

Still no answer.

Susan lifted her fist yet again. A split second before she brought it down, the door opened.

For a moment, time seemed to crystallize. Kyle stood in the doorway, staring at her with bloodshot eyes. He'd obviously just showered. His hair was damp and the well-toned contours of his torso were spangled with beads of moisture. The only thing between him and total nudity was a white towel knotted low on his hips.

That he was shocked to see her was plain. But there was another dimension to his reaction as well. Susan caught a glimpse of something—disgust? despair?—lurking behind his stunned expression.

He swore. The expletive seemed to erupt out of the very depths of his soul. Then, before Susan had a chance to speak, he started to turn away.

Goaded by feelings that had been bottled up inside her for more than eleven years, Susan shouldered her way into H.G.'s house. She stopped short a few steps inside the door when she realized there was a woman standing about six feet away. She registered a few basic details. Red hair. Green eyes. A very put-upon expression.

"Now, what?" the redhead demanded.

Kyle cursed again. He turned to Susan. "Look, I know why you've come," he said tightly. "I'm sorry about what happened with Charlie. I never expected him to show up here. I didn't realize he thought I'd promised to meet him at the arcade. Yesterday afternoon, when I dropped him off at your house, he asked me if I had any plans for today. I said something about maybe hanging out and playing video games for a few hours this morning. *That's all.* But then something came up—"

"Oh, I'll just bet it did!" Susan spat at him, glancing pointedly below his waist.

"I wouldn't, if I were you," the redhead interpolated.

"Jenna!" Kyle said, slicing a look at the other woman.

"Fine," the redhead huffed. "If that's what you want." Pivoting, she flounced out of the room.

There was a brief and brutal silence. Susan saw Kyle open his mouth to say something. She refused to let him get started.

Speaking with scathing fluency, she proceeded to tell Kyle Lochner Gordon exactly what she thought of him. She excoriated every detail of his character. She shredded his manners, his morals and his relentlessly adolescent mind-set. She condemned his car and the irresponsible way he drove it. She lambasted him for lying to Charlie about Mike's "wild and crazy" behavior in high school. Every negative thought she'd ever had about him came pouring out of her mouth.

"One week ago," she said, her voice vibrating with rage, "you told me you cared about my son. You said you'd never do anything to hurt him. Bull! Do you have any idea what you did to Charlie this morning? Do you *care* that he came home crying because of you?"

"Susan—" It was the first time he'd managed to get a word in since the redhead's exit. His voice was strained. His face had gone ashen.

"Shut up!" She wasn't going to give him a chance to weasel out of this. She wouldn't listen to his excuses or be swayed by his faked vulnerability. "I don't want to hear some sob story about what a tough time you've had since your accident. So you were washed out of the Air Force. So your days of being Hotdog King of the Cockpit are over. Well, I'm sorry, but there are a hell of a lot worse things in life than finding out you can't fly anymore. Things like sitting in a doctor's office and being told you've got terminal cancer! Things like watching s-someone you love d-dying by inches in what...in what should be the p-prime of his l-life!"

She whirled away from Kyle then, fearing she was going to break down completely. She stumbled to the front door and managed to get it open.

"Susan, please—"

Susan turned back. "I want you to stay away from my son. I want you to stay away from me. Do you understand? We don't need you. We don't want you. We don't like you!"

"Susan—"

"I've only got two words to say to you, Kyle. Grow up!"

Kyle had no idea how long he stood there staring at the inside of his uncle's front door after Susan stormed out. However long it was, it offered him more than enough time to replay every one of the things she'd said to him at least three times.

He felt . . . God, he didn't know what he was feeling. Except ashamed. Utterly, absolutely ashamed.

Create enough crap and eventually somebody will have the guts to rub your nose in it, the voice inside his skull said very quietly.

"Fan of yours, Kyle?" a feminine voice asked from a few feet in back of him.

He started at the sound, then turned around. "Yeah," he told Jenna Bradley, the NASA scientist his uncle had suggested didn't sound "too bright" on the telephone. "One of my biggest."

"I could tell." Jenna moved toward him. One corner of Kyle's mind noted that she'd gotten dressed. "I take it that was the mother of the boy who showed up earlier?"

Kyle nodded.

"Has anyone ever talked to you like that before?"

Only the damned voice inside my skull, Kyle thought mordantly.

"No," he said aloud.

"Mmm." Jenna ran a finger up Kyle's bare chest and slanted him a provocative look. "Do you want me to massage your bruised ego?"

Kyle didn't respond to her caressing touch. Not even a quiver. After a moment, he captured her hand with his own and lifted it off his body.

"Thanks," he said flatly. "But no thanks."

"I can make you feel better about yourself."

He almost smiled. "No, I don't think so."

"Are you sure?"

"Positive." Kyle understood that Jenna was his for the taking at that moment. He also understood that he wouldn't take her even if he wanted to—which he definitely didn't.

"Why not?"

"I'd just be using you, Jenna."

She looked astonished. "So? I wouldn't mind. I mean, well, frankly, Kyle, you 'use' better than any guy I know."

It was meant to be a compliment. Kyle had no doubts about that. Yet it affected him like salt on an open wound.

Jenna seemed to sense something of what he was feeling. Her expression changed. "Oh," she said very softly. "So it's like that, is it?"

Kyle blinked. "Like what?"

"You'll find out," came the enigmatic response. Jenna fluffed her flame-colored curls for a few moments. "Look, it's obvious my coming here wasn't such a hot idea. Why don't I get my things together and be on my merry way? We can pretend we said our final farewells out in California."

"Sounds like a good plan," Kyle concurred. Impelled by a need he couldn't explain, he started to turn back toward the front door.

"Kyle?"

He glanced over his shoulder. "Yeah?"

"You used to be one of the best times around, you know."

Kyle looked at the front door, snatches of Susan's emotion-filled denunciation echoing through his brain. "I used to be a lot of things," he murmured. "Now I've got to work out what I am."

Five

_____

"What do you want?" Susan asked a little more than an hour later. Her words came out like ice chips—sharply edged and freezing cold.

"I'd like to speak with Charlie," Kyle told her. He was prepared to accept anything Susan wanted to dish out. He'd half expected her to slam the door in his face. That she hadn't seemed like cause for hope.

"No." She shook her head. "I don't think so."

"Please, Susan." He'd beg if he had to. There was almost nothing he wouldn't do at this moment to set things right.

"Why?"

It was a challenge. Kyle suspected that if he failed to give a satisfactory answer, Susan might very well decide to slam the door in his face, after all.

"I need to apologize to him. It's important."

"Important?" Her brows went up. "To whom? To Charlie? To the ten-year-old boy you told to go away and leave you alone?"

"Yes, to Charlie," Kyle replied, flinching inwardly as she repeated the command he'd given her son. Then, because he'd vowed to tell the unvarnished truth, he added, "And it's important to me, too, Susan. Very important. Please. Let me talk with him. You can be there. You can listen to every word I say and you can tell me to shut up any time you want. And I will. I give you my word."

She stared at him without speaking for several long moments, her expression making it obvious she put little stock in his pledge. He sustained her gaze with all the honesty in his soul, willing her to understand how much this meant, how greatly it mattered.

Kyle knew, to the instant, when Susan made up her mind. His body tightened in anticipation of her response, bracing for rejection.

"You can come in," she said. "I'll tell Charlie you're here and want to speak to him. But if he doesn't want to see you, that's it."

"I understand."

Kyle Lochner Gordon had done some tough things in his life. But few of them had tested his mettle as painfully as waiting in Susan Brooks's homey living room to learn whether or not her son would agree to talk to him.

The relief he felt when Charlie finally walked in was almost overwhelming. But relief gave way to a sickening sense of guilt when he saw the closed-off expression on the youngster's face. He felt like a vandal.

He'd taken advantage of Charlie. He'd abused the boy's trust and fed off his innocent admiration like a parasite. But now the kid saw him for what he really was. A careless, manipulating fake. A self-centered, empty-hearted phony. The trust was destroyed, the admiration gone.

I'm sorry, kid, Kyle thought. *I'm so, so sorry.*

He watched Charlie look up at Susan, then give a little nod. Susan responded with a nod of her own.

"I'm going to go out to the kitchen now, Charlie," she said quietly. Kyle knew her words were meant to warn him, as well as to reassure her son.

"Okay, Mom."

Susan nailed Kyle with a look, then exited the room with a graceful stride. She left an awful, awkward silence in her wake.

"I guess you're pretty mad at me, huh, Charlie?" Kyle finally said.

Charlie met his eyes for the first time since coming into the living room. He shrugged his narrow shoulders. "No big deal."

Kyle had anticipated a show of anger and braced himself for it. This indifference was much, much worse. "Oh, I think it is," he countered, his throat tight. "That's why I told your mom I needed to talk to you."

Charlie cocked his chin. "I thought about it, and I remembered you didn't promise you were going to meet me at the video arcade this morning," he stated flatly. "You just said you might. I was stupid to think you'd come."

"No, Charlie. You weren't."

"Well, then, I was stupid to go over to your house."

"No, buddy—"

"Don't call me that!" The boy's rejection of the word was fierce, a reflection of the depth of his hurt.

Kyle let a few seconds tick by. "You're right," he acknowledged. "I shouldn't call you 'buddy' if I'm not going to treat you like one, should I? That's a form of lying."

Charlie blinked rapidly several times, then snuffled loudly. "I thought you *l-liked* m-me," he said, suddenly sounding very vulnerable.

"I do," Kyle assured him. "I do like you, Charlie. I didn't realize how much until I screwed up so badly this morning. I'm sorry for that, kid. I'm as sorry as I've ever been in my life. What I did was . . ." He paused, trying to put the words together.

His mouth twisted with a touch of self-mockery. "I practiced this apology about ten times while I was heading over here," he confessed. "I had plenty of time to rehearse, because I drove under the speed limit."

Charlie made a sound that was half choke, half chuckle. "No way. You never go that slow."

"Well, I did today." Kyle raked his hands back through his hair, grateful for the slight easing in the boy's hostility. "Look.

There's nothing that can excuse what I've done. But will you let me try to explain why I've acted like such a . . . jerk?''

Charlie weighed this request in a manner that reminded Kyle very much of Susan. "Okay," he eventually assented.

"Can we sit down on the couch?"

Another few moments of consideration. "Yeah. All right."

Kyle gave himself a couple of seconds to muster his resources and summon his nerve once they got settled. He knew he had just one shot at getting this right.

"You're really good at science, aren't you, Charlie?" he finally asked.

The boy looked surprised. When he replied, there was a hint of caution in his voice. "Yeah."

"Straight A's?"

"Mostly. I almost always get hundreds on my tests. I might get accelerated next year."

"In other words, you know you're an ace."

"Well, I don't go around *bragging* about it or anything."

"Oh, I realize that," Kyle said quickly. "But you don't need to brag, do you? Because everyone knows you're the best. I mean, you won a special-achievement award at this year's state science fair. And you were picked to go to science camp this summer. Just the other day, when you met my uncle, he said he remembered reading about you in the local newspaper. So people know you're good, Charlie. Isn't that right?"

Charlie squirmed, obviously torn between pride in his accomplishments and an unwillingness to seem too full of himself. "Pretty much. Yeah."

"And the guys you hang out with at school. Don't they admire you for being a whiz at science? Don't they wish they could do the stuff you do?"

Charlie grimaced. "Sometimes they call me a stuck-up geekasaurus."

"That's jealousy," Kyle assured him. "They wouldn't say things like that if they didn't know how smart you are. Now. Tell me. How do you feel when you really nail a science problem? Do you feel good?"

A nod. "Sure."

"Do you feel . . . great?"

Another nod. More emphatic than the previous one. "Yeah."

"Do you feel like you're a real hotshot? Like you can do almost *anything* you want to in the world?"

"Yeah!" The intensity of Charlie's answer matched that of Kyle's question. For a moment, his young face shone with excitement. Then he seemed to recall the content of the discussion. The light faded from his expression. He wrinkled his forehead. "What does that have to do with—?"

"Suppose you woke up one morning and you found out you could never do science again," Kyle interrupted. "Never. Ever."

"You mean, like, what if I woke up retarded or something?"

"Not exactly." Kyle paused, grappling with words and phrases. He'd always been glib. Quick with a quip, ready with the wise-guy repartee. But this required a lot more than glibness.

"Supposing you woke up able to do every single thing you can do now *except* science," he elaborated. "All of a sudden—" he snapped his fingers "—it's totally out of your reach. No matter what you do, no matter how hard you work or pray or wish, you can't do science. But you can *remember* what it was like when you could, Charlie. You can remember how great it felt to solve problems. You can remember the rush you got when you finished up a test and knew, just knew, you'd scored a hundred. You can remember every detail so vividly it's like living the experience all over again. And there's more. Everybody—your mom, your teachers, all your friends—remembers how you used to be the best at science, too. And when you see them looking at you, you get this feeling they're comparing the old you to the new one. You get the feeling they don't think you're worth very much anymore. Why should they? You don't think you're worth very much anymore, either."

Charlie stared at Kyle, gnawing his lower lip, obviously thinking things through. "Is that what happened to you?" he asked tentatively. "I don't mean not being able to be good at science anymore. But you were a really great pilot, right? And you were an astronaut, too. But because of that accident you had, you can't ever fly again. Only...only you *remember,* don't you? You remember what it was like to be a great pilot. The way you talk about it, you have to! And besides *you* remembering, other people remember, don't they? Like, right here in Wilder's Forge. Everybody knows who you are and what you used to be."

Kyle nodded. "Flying was my gift. It was all I wanted to do. It was everything I was. Or at least, everything I thought I was. Which doesn't say a lot for me as a human being. But I basically figured that as long as I was flying high, nothing else really mattered. I saw myself as being above it all. The King of the Cockpit. Mr. Hot Stuff Astronaut. And when I lost my gift, I went down. I went down hard. What happened this morning—what you saw, what I did—was the final crash and burn."

He paused, trying to gauge his young listener's reaction. After a few seconds, he went on, "I think you're a very special person, Charlie. You deserve better than having somebody like me take advantage of you. Because that's what I did. I took advantage of the fact that you looked up to me as some kind of hero. I . . . used . . . you. And the really bad thing is, I didn't realize I was doing it. I didn't realize because I wasn't thinking about anybody but myself and how bad I felt."

There was a silence.

"Do you really think I'm special, Kyle?" Charlie finally asked.

Kyle's breath caught at the top of his throat. It was the first time since they'd begun speaking that the boy had addressed him by name.

"Yes," he answered tightly. "I really think you're special."

"What you did was crummy. It was totally crummy. And it made me mad. Madder than I've ever been at anybody."

"I know that, Charlie. If I could take it back, I would. But I can't. All I can say is, I'm sorry. I'm very, very sorry."

There was another silence. Heavier than the one before.

"Okay," Charlie said at last, looking Kyle squarely in the face. "I accept your apology."

Speaking was a struggle. "Thanks."

"You . . . want to shake on it?"

No longer trusting his voice, Kyle nodded and extended his right hand. Charlie took it. They shook.

An instant later, Kyle caught a movement on the edge of his field of vision and turned his head. His heart missed a beat as he realized Susan was standing in the doorway that led from the living room to the kitchen.

He had no idea how long she'd been there. He only knew that the expression on her lovely, heart-shaped face was very different from the one he'd seen just before she'd made her exit. Her soft pink lips were slightly parted and there was a suspicious sheen in her long-lashed brown eyes. She was staring at him as though she wasn't quite certain who he was.

Their eyes met. Kyle felt his heart miss a second beat, then a third.

"Kyle?" Charlie asked, apparently oblivious to his mother's presence.

"Yeah?"

"Did my mom come to see you? Before you came here to apologize, I mean."

Kyle saw Susan flush. A hint of defensiveness entered her posture. After a moment, he turned his gaze back to Charlie.

"Yeah," he affirmed simply. "She did."

"Was she . . . mad?"

"She was angry about what I did to you, Charlie."

The boy's forehead pleated with concern. "Mom doesn't get mad very often. But when she does, she sometimes says stuff she doesn't mean."

Kyle reached out and ruffled the boy's hair. "That may be so. All I can say is everything she said to me was true—and I needed to hear it."

He didn't have to look to know that Susan had left the doorway and returned to the kitchen. He could feel her absence to the center of his soul.

Susan sensed Kyle's presence the instant he stepped into the kitchen. It didn't matter that he'd entered without a sound. It didn't matter that she had her back to the doorway and couldn't see him. She *knew* he was there with every fiber of her being.

"Where's Charlie?" she asked, staring down at the drawer of cutlery she'd just opened. She'd had a very good reason for opening it. Given time, she might remember what it was.

"Back in his room. I told him I needed a couple of minutes to talk with you. He seemed to think that was a pretty good idea."

At least ten seconds ticked by.

"I didn't mean to eavesdrop," Susan said at last.

"Of course you did." The contradiction was quick, but not at all accusatory. "I would have been surprised if you hadn't."

"You expected me to listen?" Her tone was stiff. So was her spine.

"Yes."

Susan moistened her lips, knowing Kyle had stepped closer. "You . . . wanted me to hear?"

"Absolutely."

She sensed him moving closer still. In another moment or two, he'd be standing right behind her. She shut the cutlery drawer with a bang. Taking a deep breath, she turned around.

"Why?" she demanded. Less than ninety minutes before, she'd told this man that neither she nor her son needed, wanted or liked him. She'd meant it. Without reservation. Yet after witnessing the apology he'd offered and the explanation he'd made . . . Lord, it had been so much easier when she'd been angry with him!

He lifted his tawny brows as though the answer to her question must be obvious. "Because your opinion matters to me, Susan."

Susan felt herself color. "M-my opinion . . . ?"

"Does that surprise you?"

She was too unsettled to speak anything but the truth. "Yes. Of course it does. Very much."

An emotion she couldn't identify flickered across Kyle's features. "You're honestly surprised that your opinion matters to me?"

Her mind darted back to the encounter she and Kyle had had the previous weekend. She recalled her impression that he'd been hurt when she'd accused him of carelessness. She also recalled her later suspicion that he might have been shamming.

"Does it? Really?" She wondered if her voice sounded as strange to him as it did to her.

If it did, he gave no sign. All he said was, "Yes."

"But... *why?*" They were back to square one again.

She waited tensely. Kyle looked down, developing a sudden interest in the kitchen's linoleum floor. She saw the small muscles of his well-defined jawline fret.

"Kyle?"

He lifted his gaze to meet hers once again. The look in his sky-colored eyes was half little-boy-bewildered, half something she couldn't begin to interpret. But something about that "something" sent a very female quiver skittering up her spine. No, she thought. No. I don't want to feel like this. Not about this man. He's all wrong for me!

"I don't know," he said. "I only know that it does."

Susan swallowed. "I didn't ask to have my opinion matter to you."

Kyle laughed humorlessly. "I realize that. I didn't ask to have it matter to me, either."

"So ignore it."

"I *can't.*" There was a flash of heat in his eyes. "The things you said this morning—"

"I was angry." The image of the green-eyed redhead she'd seen at H. G. Gordon's house suddenly formed in Susan's mind. She shoved the image away. She wasn't angry about the other woman. She wasn't!

Kyle touched her then. He took a step forward and cupped her shoulders with his hands. "So I noticed. But that doesn't change the fact that you were right."

She knew she ought to pull away. Or at least avert her eyes from his gaze. But she found she couldn't do either. "Right... about what?" she managed to ask.

"About me. About my life. About the fact that it's time I grew up, Susan, I—"

"And then what happened?" Ramona Bozeman demanded through a mouthful of cinnamon doughnut.

Susan ripped open a packet of artificial sweetener. She could not quite bring herself to meet her friend's eyes. "And then nothing happened."

The brunette chewed noisily for a moment, then swallowed with an audible gulp. "Let me get this straight. You're saying that you had Kyle Gordon standing in this very room, holding on to you for dear life, telling you your opinion matters to him so much he's decided to alter the entire course of his existence and *nothing happened?*"

Susan sighed wearily and dumped the packet of sweetener into a cup of coffee. Summed up in such a bare-bones fashion, the outcome of her kitchen encounter with Kyle ten days previously sounded almost as frustrating as it had actually been. "Charlie came in."

"Oh."

"He decided since he and Kyle were back to being buddies, they should go to the game arcade."

"What did Kyle do?"

"He said okay. I think he was . . . relieved at the interruption."

"And what did you do?"

"I said okay, too. And before you ask, yes, I was relieved, too."

"Things were getting a little too intense, hmm?"

"I don't know what they were getting!" Susan burst out. Slightly appalled by her emotionalism, she lifted her coffee cup and took a sip. Then she added in a more moderate tone, "Except confused."

Ramona nibbled at her doughnut. "You haven't had a chance to find out about the redhead, huh?"

"Ramona!"

"Okay. Okay." Her friend made a calming gesture. "I was just curious. At least she wasn't Wendy Marino."

Susan drank more coffee. She wasn't about to dignify the last observation by commenting on it.

"So, what's gone on with you and Kyle since the big scene? Or should I say big scenes, plural? Did you really call him a—"

"Yes," Susan cut in. "I said a lot of . . . awful things."

"Not without cause."

"Well . . ."

Ramona dropped her doughnut. "Don't tell me you've decided you were wrong about him!"

"All right, I won't."

"My God. You have!"

"No, I haven't. It's just that . . . that . . ." Susan shook her head. "Oh, I don't know! He seems . . . different."

"You can say that again. Do you know I actually passed him on the road yesterday?"

"Passed him? Do you mean while he was jogging?"

"No. Driving. I was in my car. He was in his car. The T-bird. The one the guys in shop class voted most likely to speed when we were back in high school. And I passed him."

"Oh."

"He waved at me. At us, actually. LouAnne and DeeDee were with me. They swooned."

"I can imagine."

Ramona tilted her head to one side. "You're starting to like him, aren't you, Susan."

Susan stared down at her coffee cup. "I'm starting to revise my opinion of him," she conceded reluctantly. "I've had to. I mean, the way he handled his apology to Charlie, the way he's treated him ever since . . ."

"What about the way he's treated you?"

Defenses began to slam up. "What about it?"

"Has he tried anything?"

"No!" Susan thought back to the night of her son's "rite of passage" over the porcelain bowl. Her heart skipped a beat. Her pulse rate sped up.

"Later," Kyle had said to her that night, his voice soft, his fingers stroking. She'd trembled at his touch. Tingled at his tone.

Later.

The word had been so tantalizing. So . . . troubling. It had implied everything imaginable, yet promised nothing absolute.

"Susan?"

Susan started. "I don't know why you think Kyle Gordon would try anything with me."

Ramona rolled her eyes. "Oh, puh-leeze. Do you honestly believe Charlie is the main attraction for Kyle around this place?"

Susan took a gulp of her now lukewarm coffee. "I'm not his type, Ramona."

"Is he yours?"

"I think we've covered this territory already."

"True. But that was before you told me you'd had a dream about him wearing silver lamé underwear with a lightning bolt on the crotch."

Susan choked. She'd known she'd regret confessing that bizarre dream to Ramona. "They were made of aluminum foil." She put down the coffee cup. "And I never said anything about where the lightning bolt was."

"Give me a break. Where else would it be?" A small frown. "Well, okay. Maybe on the tush. Kyle does have one of the cutest—"

"Enough, Ramona."

There was a pause. Susan studied the inside of her coffee cup. Finally she sighed. "Do you want to know the worst thing? It's pretty bad."

"Hey, I'm a high-school guidance counselor. I can take it."

Susan sighed again. She lifted her gaze and looked at her friend. "I was almost glad when Kyle did what he did to Charlie."

Ramona's brows shot up.

"I don't mean I wasn't angry. And I certainly didn't want my son to be hurt the way he was. But..."

"But?"

"I felt this horrible sense of validation, Ramona. This really nasty sense of satisfaction that I'd been right all along about Kyle."

"In other words, you thought it would be the end of any attraction you might feel toward him. That you could file him under 'total creep' and forget about him."

A fourth sigh. "Yes."

"And now?"

Susan made a helpless gesture. "I'm so *confused*. Listening to the things he said when he apologized to Charlie ... I mean, oh, all right! I'll admit it. I'd made up my mind that Kyle's feelings about flying were just as adolescent as all his other feelings seemed to be. But, God, Ramona. The way he talked about not being able to fly anymore. The look on his face! I couldn't believe the hurt I heard. The hurt I saw. I found myself wondering what *I'd* do if I loved something that much and lost it."

"But you have."

"W-what?"

"You loved Mike. You lost him."

Susan went rigid with shock. "That's not the same—"

"No. It's not the same thing," Ramona cut in. "Not exactly. But there *is* a similarity, Susan. I think one of the reasons you're feeling so confused right now is that you've started to face the fact that you've got a lot in common with Kyle. You've both had very important parts of your lives stolen from you. And you're both having problems dealing with it."

Susan didn't know how to respond to this. Or if she did, she wasn't able to bring herself to do so. Finally, after a long silence, she asked, "So...where am I supposed to go from here?"

Ramona reached across the kitchen table and patted her hand. "Wait until Charlie goes off to camp. You'll think of something."

"Underwear?" Charlie pronounced the word as though he had only a vague notion of what it meant.

Susan refrained from rolling her eyes in exasperation. But she was tempted. Brother, was she tempted!

This was the day Charlie was supposed to depart for the Science Academy summer camp he'd been selected to attend. As part of her ongoing effort to demonstrate that she recognized he was growing up, she'd allowed her son to pack his own gear. She had, however, reserved the right to inspect his suitcases.

"Yes, Charlie," she said, willing herself to be patient. She surveyed the three lumpy-looking pieces of canvas luggage sitting on Charlie's bed. The largest of them had a goiterlike bulge on one side. "Underwear. The white cotton things you wear under your clothes."

"I *know* what underwear is, Mom."

"I'm thrilled to hear it. Did you pack any?"

Charlie fiddled with his glasses. "I stuck in a couple of pairs."

"A couple of pairs?" Susan crossed to the bed. "You're going to be gone for two weeks."

"So? I can do laundry. I have soap. Or I can wear my swimming trunks. Kyle says that's what him and Dad used to do when they went camping."

"That's *he* and Dad, not him and Dad," Susan corrected, conscious that resentment was no longer the dominant emotion she felt when her son said Kyle's name. What the dominant emotion was, she wasn't ready to say. "And I don't care if the two of them used to dance around stark naked on Main Street. *You* are going to wear underwear while you're away, Charles Michael Brooks. And it's *not* going to be the same underwear for fourteen days running."

"Aw, Mom!"

Susan unzipped the top of the smallest bag. She decided she'd work her way up to the goiter. She winnowed through the contents, satisfying herself that they included at least some of the items her son needed.

She moved on to the second bag. "Ye gods!" she exclaimed. "You must have every computer disk you own in here. Do you really need all of these?"

"Of course I really need all of them," came the inevitable and slightly indignant response. "Kyle's uncle let me make copies of some of his SETI files. You know, the ones about his work on searching the skies for alien transmissions? He says I can show his stuff to the guys at camp. Like, maybe, they'll pick up on something he hasn't. But I don't think so. H.G. is wicked smart."

"True," Susan acknowledged. "And it was generous of him to share his, ah, alien files with you." Steeling herself for the worst, she proceeded to the bag with the mysterious bulge.

"You don't have to check that one, Mom," Charlie said, moving hastily to her side. "I put in everything I was supposed to. But I didn't do..."

Susan already had the bag unzipped. She peered inside and let out a groan of dismay.

"...a really careful packing job."

Susan started to empty the piece of luggage, marveling at her son's capacity for understatement. "These clothes were freshly washed and pressed when I gave them to you, young man. How in the name of—" She broke off as she discovered the cause of the bulge. It was a silvery sphere, about the size of a melon. "Just what is *this* supposed to be?" she demanded, lifting the item out with both hands.

Charlie shifted uneasily. "It's my Bliss Ball."

Susan stiffened, images of religious cults, weird role-playing fantasy games and—heaven help her—hallucinogenic drugs swirling through her mind. She tightened her grip on the metallic globe.

Was it possible? she asked herself worriedly. The news was full of stories about children Charlie's age and younger getting caught up in all sorts of unsavory things. What if...?

Susan looked down at the object she was clutching. Her reflection—distorted by the curved plane of the mirror-smooth surface—gazed back. An odd sensation rippled through her body. She exhaled suddenly, the tension-bunched muscles in her neck and shoulders relaxing.

No, she thought, her anxiety melting like ice in summer. Not my Charlie. I'd know if he'd gotten mixed up in something that wasn't good for him. And if I didn't know...Kyle certainly would.

"What did you call this?" she asked after a few seconds, looking at her son. She stroked the globe, intrigued by its sleekness. The object seemed remarkably light for its size, as though it might be hollow.

"My Bliss Ball," Charlie said again. "I found it when I was foolin' around up in Cumming's Meadow. It was a couple of days before I met Kyle. I showed it to you when I brought it home, Mom. Don't you remember? You were fixin' supper. You said, 'That's very interesting. Now go wash your hands.'"

Susan frowned, trying to recall the incident just described. She couldn't. Her failure wasn't really a surprise. Charlie was an inveterate collector. He was always picking up odds and ends, bits and pieces, and lugging them home. The truth was, she didn't pay very much attention to what he scrounged.

"Why 'Bliss Ball,' Charlie?" It was an unlikely name for a youngster—even one as bright as her son—to pick. Yet it seemed peculiarly fitting to Susan.

Charlie shrugged. "I don't know. Because it feels good to hold, I guess. I'm not even sure what it is. But it's cool."

Susan set the object down on the bed. "Well, be that as it may, I don't think Bliss Balls are on the list of things to pack for science camp."

"But, Mom—"

"But, nothing," she snapped, her irritation about his luggage returning. She glanced at her watch and grimaced. "Let's get these bags straightened out. I want to be ready to hit the road in thirty minutes."

A little more than an hour later, Kyle Gordon found out what it was like to have Susan Brooks welcome his arrival at her home with open arms.

Metaphorically speaking, of course.

Charlie came dashing out of the house almost as soon as he pulled up in front of it. "Kyle! Kyle!"

"Hi, kid," Kyle called back, shutting off the T-bird's engine and setting the brake. He opened the door and got out. He stretched skyward, then shoved the sunglasses he was wearing up on top of his head. He squinted against the dazzling noonday sun.

"I can't believe you're here!" Charlie declared, reaching the side of the car. His face was flushed and there was an agitated look in his eyes.

"The meeting I had in Connecticut got canceled at the last minute, so I turned around and headed back to Wilder's Forge," Kyle explained, assessing the youngster's demeanor with a touch of concern. "What's with you? I thought you'd be long gone to your science camp by now."

"Mom's car is dead."

"Dead?" Kyle glanced toward the station wagon sitting in the driveway. While he'd been aware that Susan was having a few problems with it, there'd been no indication those problems were terminal.

Charlie nodded. "Completely."

"Has your mom called a mechanic?"

"About a hundred of them. They all say they're too busy to come out today. Now she's trying to get taxi service."

"Forget that," Kyle said instantly. "I'll drive you myself."

Charlie's eyes went wide. "You will? Really?"

"Sure. No problem."

"Oh, wow! Thanks!"

At that moment, the front door of the house opened again and Susan stepped out. "Charlie—"

Her son turned. "Mom! Mom! Everything's okay!" he yelled. "Kyle says he'll drive me to camp!"

Kyle experienced what had become a very familiar stirring in his body as he watched Susan's approach. While he'd seen sexier walks in his life—everything from hip-swinging sashays to sultry strolls—he'd never seen a more womanly one. Susan didn't flaunt what she had. Indeed, he was still trying to figure out whether she was aware of just how much she had to show off. But the allure was there: innate, oddly innocent and owing nothing to artifice.

She was wearing a red-and-white shirtwaist dress that skidded to a halt about an inch above her knees. The softly tailored style suited her compact yet curvy figure. The fine pinstripe pattern of the summery fabric made Kyle think of peppermint sticks. And peppermint sticks made him think of—

Brakes on, he ordered himself sharply. This is Mike Brooks's widow. This is Charlie Brooks's mother. This is also the woman who reamed you out like there was no tomorrow two weeks ago. You're in her life on a probationary pass, on a temporary basis. So cool your jets.

It was easier said than done, but Kyle did it the same way he'd been doing it for the past fourteen days. Breath by breath, pulse by pulse, he clamped down on his desire for a woman who was out of his league in every way that really mattered.

Susan came to a halt just within touching distance. A breeze fingered her glossy brown hair, sending a lock of it unfurling across her face. She brushed the errant strands away with a quick swipe of her hand.

Kyle shifted his weight from one foot to the other. He knew the feel of Susan's hair. He'd learned the silken luxury of it weeks before, on the night she'd called him careless and he'd come within a heartbeat of kissing her for the first time. Even now, the tactile memory of it tantalized his fingertips. Maybe someday...

Yeah. Right. And maybe someday he'd run in the Kentucky Derby.

"This is very kind of you, Kyle," Susan said. The smile she offered him was as warm as the weather.

"My pleasure." Kyle thrust his hands into the pockets of his trousers and rocked back on his heels.

"I'll go get my stuff, Kyle," Charlie announced. "Then you and me can take off. Okay?"

Kyle saw a flicker of hurt cross Susan's face. He looked at the boy. "No. Not okay. Number one, it's you and *I*. And number two, my offer of a ride includes your mother."

"But I thought—"

"I know what you thought. Your mother's coming with us. Now move out. Go get your gear."

Charlie hesitated, plainly thinking about arguing the point. But after glancing from Kyle to his mother and back again, he capitulated with a shrug and dashed off toward the house.

"You keep that Bliss Ball out of your luggage, young man!" Susan called after him.

"Bliss Ball?" Kyle questioned when she turned back to face him. Lord, he liked the way she was smiling at him! "What's a Bliss Ball?"

"Just this—" Susan sketched a spherical shape with her hands "—thing Charlie picked up someplace and brought home. Part of his endlessly expanding collection of junk."

Kyle nodded his comprehension. "I was a pack rat when I was a kid, too."

"Really?"

"Still am, in a way. One of the things I've discovered since I came back to Wilder's Forge is that my uncle saved boxes and boxes of my stuff." He paused, suddenly thinking about the Orb. H.G. had become quite attached to the object in the past few weeks. He claimed it stimulated his creativity. "H.G. has a theory that you never really need anything until after you throw it out."

Susan laughed. "That sounds like the theory of a man who has much more storage space than I do. One of the things I plan to do while Charlie is away is cull through the clutter in his room."

"Big job?"

"Huge."

"Well, holler if you need help. I may not be good for much, but I've got a real talent for heavy lifting."

Susan gave him an odd look. "Thank you. I . . . I just might do that."

"Good."

There was a brief pause. Kyle took one hand out of his pocket and forked his fingers back through his hair. The breeze shifted. He caught the faint floral scent of Susan's perfume.

"I appreciate your willingness to drive Charlie to camp," she finally said, fiddling with fabric of her dress.

"You're not planning to go with us?" Kyle was startled by the degree of disappointment he felt.

"Well . . ." Susan glanced toward the house.

"Look, I know Charlie would like this to be a guys-only road trip. He's probably uptight about saying goodbye to you in front of a lot of people. But I'd like you to come along, Susan. Please."

She studied him for several seconds. Kyle began to wonder if he'd made his request sound too urgent. He couldn't seem to find the right tone with Susan. While there'd been moments during the past two weeks when he'd sensed her reaching out to him, there'd been many others when she'd pulled back behind defenses he was still trying to gauge.

"Come on." He put a wicked little spin on the words, deciding to see if he could stir her up a bit. "Let me take you for a ride."

Susan's chin ratcheted up a notch. A tinge of color entered her cheeks.

That's right, Kyle thought. *You know I'm trying to con you. Now call me on it.*

She did.

"Do you promise to keep both hands on the wheel?" Susan's tone had a tart-sweet edge, like perfectly made lemonade.

"Oh, absolutely. And at least one eye on the road at all times."

"What's the other eye going to be doing?"

Kyle bit back the impulse to say it was going to be watching her. "Checking for speed traps," he replied after a moment.

Susan nibbled her lower lip, obviously stringing him along. "I *suppose* it sounds safe enough."

Kyle suddenly remembered something. "It may be even safer than you think," he declared, giving her a deliberately cocky wink. "I've got some new equipment in the T-bird I've been wanting you to check out."

"And just what might this new equipment be?"

He turned on the Gordon Grin. "Seat belts."

Six

The sky overhead was a cloudless blue. The road unfurling in front was free of traffic. The woman sitting barely two feet away from him was Susan. Kyle Lochner Gordon decided life was looking pretty good.

The purr of the powerful engine under the Thunderbird's scarlet hood and the soar of Aretha Franklin's soulful voice coming from the dashboard tape player seemed to underscore this assessment.

All he needed now was—

"It was your idea, wasn't it, Kyle?"

Kyle shifted gears and slanted a quick glance to his right. Susan was smiling at him. There was softness in her dark eyes that had a decidedly disruptive effect on his pulse rate.

"What?" he asked, returning his gaze to the road. They'd been on the road home for about ninety minutes. Although they'd chitchatted casually during the first part of the journey, they'd lapsed into a companionable silence about twenty miles back. He had no idea what train of thought had led to Susan's question.

"Charlie hugging me goodbye when we got ready to leave him at camp."

Kyle resisted the temptation to look to his right again. "What makes you say that?"

"Because left to his own devices, my son probably would have shaken my hand."

"You didn't mind the hug, did you?"

"M-mind?" There was a tiny tremor in her voice. "No. Of course not. I was...surprised. And t-touched."

Kyle stayed silent for a minute, recalling the conversation he'd had with Charlie as they'd stood in the parking lot of the science camp. Susan had gone off in search of a lavatory in preparation for the trip back.

"Will you check up on my mom while I'm gone, Kyle?" the kid had asked.

"Sure thing, buddy," he'd answered.

"You don't have to hang out with her a lot or anything. Un-less...like, uh, you *want* to. I mean, uh, you remember that time we talked about you maybe, uh, asking her out on a...a..."

"Uh-huh."

"Do you think you might?"

He'd sidestepped the question. "Would it be all right with you if I did?"

"Yeah."

"Okay. We'll see."

There'd been a pause. Kyle had leaned up against the side of his car and folded his arms, savoring the warmth of the day and contemplating the drive ahead. He'd thought about watching Susan in the rearview mirror on the ride up. She'd crossed her legs at one point, causing the hemline of her dress to go from knee-brushing to thigh-baring. Only his pilot's reflexes had saved him from doing something really stupid with the car in reaction to the sudden display of skin.

"Do you think she's going to hug me goodbye in front of everybody?" Charlie had queried anxiously after nearly a minute.

Kyle had lowered his gaze, not really surprised by the question. "I'd say that's a distinct possibility."

"What would happen if I told her not to?"

"I think she'd be hurt."

Charlie had fidgeted, plainly finding this idea unpalatable. "I guess I'll have to take it like a man, then."

Kyle had hidden a smile. "Maybe you should try hugging her first."

"Huh?"

"A preemptive strike. Your mom won't be expecting you to hug her, right? And if you do, she'll probably be so paralyzed with surprise she won't be able to embarrass you with any mushy stuff."

Charlie's mouth had dropped open. He'd stared at Kyle with something close to awe. "What a great idea!"

"Well," Kyle began mildly, coming out of his reverie, "I may have suggested something that gave him the—" He stopped, hearing a choky little sound coming from his right.

Easing off on the gas pedal, he glanced to the side again. Susan's face was now partially averted, her expression obscured by her wind-tossed hair.

"Susan?" He darted a look at the road ahead, then returned his gaze to the woman sitting next to him.

Susan shook her head and made a "never mind" gesture with her left hand.

"Susan, please." He slowed the car even more. "Look at me."

After a moment, she did as he'd asked. "I'm s-sorry," she apologized, meeting his gaze with wide, tear-filled eyes.

Kyle pulled over to the side of the road and braked almost before he realized what he was doing. He wasn't good with crying women. His talent for handling the opposite sex—and it was ridiculous to pretend he hadn't been born with a certain touch—was limited when it came to coping with tears. He'd always been inclined to bail out at the first sign of waterworks.

Well, he wasn't going to do that now. Not with Susan.

"Hey, it's okay," he told her, undoing his seat belt. "It's okay." Leaning over, he unhooked Susan's seat belt, too.

"I'm s-sorry," she repeated. "I know you m-must hate this, K-Kyle. But I started thinking about l-leaving Charlie...."

"No. Shhh. I understand." Slipping his arms around her, he gathered her to him. She shifted, her body curving into his. She was shaking.

"I feel l-like an idiot. But this is the f-first t-time . . ."

"I know, Susan. I know. It's okay."

"I didn't w-want to cry . . . in f-front of . . . Charlie."

"Shhh. Shhh. It's all right."

"He would . . . he would have d-died of em-embarrassment."

"It's okay. I understand. There . . . shhh."

Kyle wanted to comfort Susan. Nothing more, nothing less. And for the first few minutes, that's all he did. He held her gently while he murmured what he hoped were suitably soothing words and stroked the silken disorder of her hair in what he assured himself was a completely asexual way. His efforts seemed to work, too. Gradually the trembling in her body eased, and her sobs gave way to intermittent sniffles.

He couldn't pinpoint the precise moment when his desire to comfort became something more combustible. He only knew the transformation occurred. His awareness of the woman he was embracing altered and escalated.

The fragrant scent of Susan's skin in his nostrils . . .

Sweet.

The teasing fan of her breath through the cotton of his shirt . . .

Soft.

The fullness of her breasts, pressing against his forearm . . .

Sensuous.

His body started to harden. His blood began to heat. His mind hazed with a yearning that was more than eleven years old.

Susan, he thought. *Oh, Susan . . .*

She sensed the change in him. She must have. For one heart-stopping instant, Kyle thought his desire had become hers, as well. He felt her quiver. He heard her say something—his name?—in a throaty whisper.

And then she lifted her head and looked at him. Her eyes had gone very dark. There was almost no distinction between the brown irises and black pupils.

The shimmer of hunger Kyle saw in Susan's eyes was almost his undoing. But in addition to the hunger he saw uncertainty. And surprise. Surprise so intense it was almost shock.

"K-Kyle?" she asked, a catch in her voice.

He had to fight to drag sufficient air into his lungs. No, he told himself fiercely. No. Forget about it, hot dog! Absolutely not.

Not here. Not now. Not this way. And not with this woman, dammit! Maybe . . . never . . . with this woman.

"Kyle?" Although her voice was steadier than it had been a few seconds before, she was starting to blush.

Struggling to keep his expression neutral, Kyle released his hold on Susan and eased away from her. "You're right," he said.

She shook her head, clearly confused. "I'm . . . about w-what?"

"Charlie would have taken it hard if you'd cried when you said goodbye to him. That's why I suggested he try hugging you first. So you'd be too stunned to, ah, get mushy."

There was a long pause. Kyle tried to make sense of the emotions he saw chasing across Susan's expressive face but failed. They came and went so quickly he could barely separate one from another, much less interpret them.

Finally Susan gave a watery chuckle. "I . . . see." She wiped beneath her eyes with her fingers, then produced a crooked little smile. "Well, your suggestion certainly worked. I'm just sorry you got stuck with the mushy—" a sniff "—stuff. I guess it was delayed reaction."

Kyle fought the urge to take her into his arms again. "No problem."

She gave another chuckle—this one drier than the first—then leaned forward and retrieved her purse from the floor. Kyle watched her open it and take out a packet of tissues.

"Better?" he asked once she'd finished blotting her face and blowing her nose. Her color was back to normal. So was his pulse, more or less.

Susan nodded, fiddling with her hair and dress. "Yes. Thank you. Much. I'm sorry if I—"

"There's nothing to be sorry for, Susan." He reached for the ignition. "Now, why don't I get you home?"

When he got her home, he asked her out to dinner.

"You mean . . . tonight?" Her surprise was palpable.

"Unless you have other plans."

"Well, no. But . . ."

"Charlie asked me to keep an eye on you while he's away."

A pause.

"He did?"

"Yeah. I told him I would."

"Oh."

Another pause.

"Well?"

"Do I have any say in this, Kyle? Or have you and my son sorted everything out between you?"

"You can have all the say you want, Susan. Try starting with yes."

A third pause, punctuated by a brief but very feminine smile. Every hormone in Kyle's body snapped to attention.

"Yes."

"No. Ugh. Lord, where did I find *this?* No, he's seen it. Yuck. Nah—uh, maybe. Ugly. Uglier! Makes me look fat. Makes me look . . ."

Susan paused in the act of culling through—and utterly condemning about ninety-five percent of—the contents of her closet.

You've lost your mind, she told herself. You've totally lost your grip on reality, and it's all because of Kyle Gordon.

He'd wanted to kiss her earlier. She'd seen it in his face. She'd heard it in his breathing. She'd felt it in his body.

She'd felt a great deal more than a desire to kiss, as a matter of fact. More than enough to have been flattered, flustered and . . . well, uh . . .

Why hadn't he? she wondered for what seemed like the zillionth time since she'd arrived home. Why hadn't Kyle kissed her when he'd so obviously wanted to?

Susan closed her eyes for a moment, conscious of a throbbing in her bloodstream, a thrumming in her brain. She felt a treacherous melting between her thighs.

She'd wanted him to kiss her. She'd wanted it so much she'd almost taken the initiative herself. But an instant before she'd worked up the nerve, he'd eased off and backed away.

Kyle's decision not to kiss her hadn't been a rejection, exactly. More like a...a...

A what? A rain check?

Her memory flashed back three weeks. Back to the night of her "nice" date with Jack Wiley. Back to the two-syllable word Kyle had said to her after that date had ended.

Later, he'd told her. *Later.*

What are you going to do if "later" turns out to be "now," tonight, Susan? she asked herself suddenly. And what are you going to do if it doesn't?

Susan opened her eyes and glared at the chaos inside her closet.

"How should I know?" she demanded with a hint of desperation. "I don't even know what I'm going to wear!"

All Kyle wanted to do was look at her. Well, no. Not all. But looking was as far as he could go while he and Susan were sitting opposite each other at a very conspicuous table in the best restaurant in Wilder's Forge.

She was wearing a simple off-the-shoulder dress made of coral-colored cotton. The style of the garment was subtle and body skimming. The fabric had just a hint of sheerness—enough to keep him wondering how much, if anything, there was between it and bare skin.

Her hair was loose, falling to her shoulders in soft waves. She'd artfully shadowed her eyelids and considerably enhanced the lushness of her lashes. Her lips were a few shades darker than her dress. Their rich coloring and ripe curves made Kyle think of sun-warmed tropical fruit.

"Is something wrong?" Susan asked, glancing up from her menu.

Kyle resisted an urge to loosen his tie. "No. Not at all. Why?"

"Well, the way you were looking at me..."

There was a glass of ice water sitting to Kyle's right. He picked it up and took a deep drink. "I was thinking how beautiful you are," he said after a moment.

"Oh." She colored.

"Do you mind?" Not for the first time, Kyle noticed that Susan's blushes involved more than her throat and face. He would have given a lot to know exactly where on her body they began.

"What? That you think I'm beautiful?"

He nodded.

Susan gave an odd laugh. The breathy sound of it feathered along Kyle's nervous system. He had the feeling Susan was reacting to a joke she wasn't going to share. "No, Kyle," she replied. "I don't mind at all."

At that point, a waiter materialized by their table and took their orders. Then there was a brief silence. Kyle toyed with the stem of his water glass. He knew Susan was watching him. He could feel the touch of her gaze. Eventually, he looked across the table at her once again. Their eyes met and mated.

"There are a couple of things I'd like to get cleared up with you," he told her after a few seconds.

Susan shifted in her seat but didn't speak.

"The first is your thinking I've lied to Charlie about Mike."

"I never—" She stopped, obviously realizing what he was referring to. "Oh. That."

"Yeah. That. Look, Susan, I want you to know I wasn't trying to do any harm—to blacken Mike's memory or anything like that. Yes, I exaggerated his part in some of the stunts we pulled when we were kids—"

"Like telling Charlie *Mike* was the one who stole the rival team's mascot on the eve of the big football game your senior year?"

It was difficult to get a fix on Susan's tone, but Kyle's principal impression was of amusement. He certainly heard no trace of the outrage she'd directed at him two weeks before.

"Mike *was* the lookout," he said. "The ransom note was his idea, too."

"Not quite as impressive as shinnying up a drainpipe to climb into a second-story window then jimmying a lock with a credit card."

"Well . . ."

"Especially not to a ten-year-old boy."

Blue eyes locked with brown. Kyle felt his pulse accelerate. "You understand why I did it?" he asked wonderingly.

Susan nodded, her dark hair swaying against her throat and shoulders. "Yes. At least, I think I do. Even when I was angriest at you, Kyle, I never believed you were trying to make Charlie think less of Mike. Besides—" her mouth curved into a tenderly rueful smile "—Mike would've loved to have been the one who went up the drainpipe. He would've loved to have done *all* the wild and crazy things you've told his son he did."

"So, you don't think I should let Charlie know...the truth?"

"No," Susan responded simply. "I don't."

Their waiter returned at this point, bringing their wine , salads and a wicker basket of hot crusty rolls. "Anything else I can do for you?" he asked.

Go away, Kyle thought. "No, thanks," he said aloud.

The waiter moved off.

Kyle took a sip of his wine. Susan took a sip of hers.

"You said there were a couple of things you wanted to get cleared up," she prompted quietly.

This time, Kyle was the one to shift his position. He was about to broach a very touchy issue. It was an issue he would have liked to avoid, but knew he couldn't.

"I need to explain about Jenna," he said finally.

Susan looked blank. "Jenna?"

"The woman you saw at H.G.'s two weeks ago. The redhead."

Susan stiffened. Hot color charged up into her cheeks then beat a hasty retreat, leaving her much paler than normal. "No," she said tightly. "That's all right. You don't need to—"

Kyle reached across the table and captured one of her hands. She tried to pull free, but he wouldn't release her.

"Susan, please," he said urgently. "I was going to explain to you in the kitchen that day, after I apologized to Charlie. But, well, you know what happened. I've been trying to find the right time ever since. I think it's important you know exactly what did—'' he took a deep breath ''—and didn't happen between Jenna and me.''

Susan went very still. Only her eyes moved, searching his face. Kyle waited. Finally, he saw her give a tiny nod. ''All right,'' she said.

Kyle let go of her hand and eased back in his seat.

''All right,'' he echoed, holding Susan's gaze. ''Jenna's a radio astronomer. She works for NASA. We had a...thing. Out in California. She's got an eye for pilots. She really likes the whole King of the Cockpit routine. And I, well, I've never said no to uncritical admiration from attractive members of the opposite sex, if you take my meaning.''

''I think so.''

''We had some good times. Nothing serious. No strings attached. Just good times. We were already drifting apart when my accident happened. I'm not entirely sure why Jenna decided to come to Wilder's Forge to see me. All I know is that when she showed up at H.G.'s front door carrying a bottle of tequila and a six-pack of beer, letting her in seemed like a dandy idea.''

''Kyle—''

''We drank some,'' Kyle went on quickly, knowing that if he let Susan break his momentum now, he'd lose his courage entirely. ''And we talked. Or, rather, *I* talked about my great glory days as a pilot and about the shuttle mission that was supposed to be mine six months down the line. I started to feel sorry for myself.'' He showed his teeth. ''You're stunned to hear that, right, Susan? I mean, you've never noticed I have this tendency to wallow in self-pity.''

''Kyle.'' This time, Susan leaned forward. ''Please—''

Again, he overrode her. ''Well, eventually, one thing led to another. At least it was *supposed* to. But when push came to shove, I couldn't do it. I couldn't...perform.'' Kyle shook his head, feeling his face darken with a uniquely male sense of humiliation. ''That was a first for me.''

Susan moistened her lips. Kyle wished she hadn't.

''If...if you'd been drinking...'' she began tentatively.

"Yeah, maybe." He'd considered this obvious explanation for his impotence, of course. But he'd come to the conclusion that the reasons for his total lack of sexual response had been a lot more complicated than too much alcohol. "Then again, maybe not. Jenna was . . . understanding. She was also pretty exhausted. She finally decided to sack out in my uncle's room. I sat up and drank. And the more I drank, the more I thought. And what I thought basically boiled down to the idea that I was worthless. I mean, God! I'd known I couldn't fly anymore. And now it looked like I couldn't—" he gestured "—either."

There was a silence.

"I'm sorry, Kyle," Susan said finally.

"No." He rejected her compassion. He had to. He'd rather have her anger than her pity. "I'm the one who's sorry. Just let me finish, okay?" He took a steadying breath. "I finally fell asleep. Or passed out. The next thing I knew, Charlie was knocking at the front door. The expression he got when he saw me. . . I couldn't handle it, Susan. I couldn't face him. So I told him to go away."

"And then I showed up."

"Yeah. And then you showed up."

"And Jenna?"

"After you got through with me, she offered to massage my bruised ego." He hesitated, then added, "I said no."

Susan lifted her glass and took a sip of wine. Kyle noticed that her hand was less than steady.

"Why?" she asked after a moment.

He hesitated again. How many times had he pondered that question? he wondered. And how many times had he come back to the same answer?

"Because it would have been wrong," he replied simply. "Even if I'd wanted her, which I didn't, it would have been wrong."

Another silence fell between them then. Kyle looked away for a few seconds. Maybe he'd just made a terrible mistake, he thought. Yet he'd seen no option but honesty. At least, no option he could permit himself to take.

Finally he looked back at the woman sitting opposite him. Her head was bowed, her face partially veiled by her dark hair.

Kyle's heart began to slam inside his chest like a hammer hitting an anvil. He experienced a split second of wooziness. He clenched his hands, battling down the disorienting sensation.

"Susan?" he asked.

She lifted her head slowly, her hair spilling back from her face. Her expression was . . . strange. In a bizarre way, it reminded Kyle of the expression she'd worn hours earlier in the car, when he'd been fighting the urge to kiss her.

"Do you want to go home?"

The question clearly caught her by surprise. Kyle watched her eyes widen and the color in her cheeks intensify. After a moment, he saw her chin notch up.

"No," came the very firm reply. "I don't."

"You . . . still want to have dinner with me?"

Her chin went up a bit more. "Yes, Kyle. I still want to—" Susan stopped abruptly, her gaze shifting from his face to something behind him. "Omigod," she breathed.

"Susan?"

"You'll never guess who just walked— No! Don't turn around."

He stiffened. "Who is it?"

"Jack Wiley."

The sound of another man's name on Susan's lips made Kyle's stomach knot. "Jack—"

"He's with Wendy Marino."

She didn't want the evening to end.

That was the conclusion Susan came to about three hours later as Kyle walked her from his car to her front door.

She had to admit that the explanation about Jenna Bradley had shaken her badly at first. And after she'd gotten over the initial shock, she'd been assailed by a sense of jealousy so intense she could taste it. Her recognition that this jealousy was unreasonable to the point of being irrational hadn't tempered the emotion one whit.

It had been a struggle, but she'd finally battled her unruly feelings into submission. What Kyle had done in the past was none of her concern. What he might do in the future—

No! She couldn't allow herself to think like that. The man hadn't even *kissed* her, for heaven's sake!

Besides, one of the things that had become very evident to her during dinner was that although Kyle Lochner Gordon apparently had stopped yearning for his yesterdays, he was still very tentative when it came to planning his tomorrows.

They reached the front door. Susan turned and looked up at her escort.

The warm summer night was crystalline clear. The moon overhead was full. The silvery illumination it provided underscored the compelling planes and hollows of Kyle's angular face.

Susan catalogued his features slowly—the strongly drawn brows, the steady eyes, the sensually sardonic mouth. His light brown hair was mussed, with a few tawny strands curving down over his forehead. She wanted to reach up and stroke them back into place but she didn't quite have the nerve.

Almost as though sensing the nature of her thoughts, Kyle suddenly raised his right hand and thrust his fingers back through his hair. A moment later, the same stubbornly errant strands flopped forward again.

"Did you mind?" he asked suddenly.

Susan blinked. "Mind...what?"

Again, the hand through the hair. This time Susan's eyes were drawn from Kyle's face to his body. He'd begun the evening impeccably dressed, including a well-tailored navy sports jacket and expensive-looking tie. He'd shed both in the car coming home. Without the camouflage of his jacket, Susan was reminded of how superbly proportioned he was—broad through the shoulders, streamlined everywhere else.

"Seeing Jack with Wendy," he specified after a second or two.

"No." She shook her head. "Why would you ask that?"

"You went out with Jack."

"Once."

"You still—" a brief jump of a jaw muscle "—like him."

Susan smoothed a hand down the front of her dress, not knowing what to make of this line of conversation. Surely Kyle couldn't seriously think that she and Jack Wiley were—

Her pulse stuttered for an instant.

Lord. Maybe he *did* think it! And if he did . . .

She'd naturally want to set him straight, wouldn't she? She wouldn't want to leave him with any wrong impressions, would she? Well . . .

Susan veiled her eyes with her lashes. "Of course I like Jack," she said.

"Of course," Kyle echoed.

Susan knew it was wrong to relish the edge she heard in his voice, but she couldn't help herself. Urged on by an unfamiliar desire to tease, she looked up once again. "Jack's a nice man, Kyle," she declared sweetly.

She was hoping to strike a spark and she did. Unfortunately it was not the kind of spark she'd been anticipating. A glint suddenly appeared in Kyle's eyes. The dimple in his right cheek indented.

"Nice?" he repeated on a questioning inflection.

"Yes." She lifted her chin, challenging him. Somewhere in the back of her mind she wondered why she was acting in such an uncharacteristic fashion. "*Very* nice."

The glint got brighter. The dimple deeper. "Glad to hear it."

"You are?"

"Mmm-hmm."

Susan narrowed her eyes. Somehow, some way, she'd just had the tables turned on her. Kyle was supposed to be . . . well, he wasn't supposed to be what he obviously was at this moment. And what he obviously was, was very sure of himself.

And of her, it would seem.

"You're glad to hear I think Jack Wiley is a very nice man?"

"Oh, yeah. Definitely."

"Why?"

"Because women don't use the adjective 'nice' about men they're attracted to."

She gasped, shocked by his smug-sounding assertion. "That's ridiculous!"

Kyle shook his head, closing most of the distance between them. "No, it's not. A guy hears the word 'nice' from a woman and he knows he hasn't got a chance in hell with her. Because sooner or later she's going to to follow the 'nice' up with a 'but' and after the 'but' she's going to say something like, 'I hope we can still be friends.'"

Susan suddenly realized that her hands were resting against Kyle's chest. She had no memory of having moved them. She told herself she was preparing to fend him off—assuming fending off became necessary.

"Has any woman ever said *you* were...nice?" she asked. In her mind, the question was supposed to be a jab at his overweening male ego. But the way it came out of her mouth...

The Gordon Grin unfurled by slow, breath-stealing increments. By the time it was completely in place, Susan was beginning to fear she might succumb to oxygen deprivation.

"Not to my face," was Kyle's provocative reply. "Are you planning to be the first?"

"N-no," she managed. "Because... I've never thought... you... you were..." Her voice trailed off as his hand came up to cup her chin. Her thoughts scattered like fallen leaves before an autumn wind.

"Good," Kyle responded huskily, lowering his head. His breath fanned her lips. "Because I'm not, Susan. I'm not nice—at all."

He began with a butterfly-light caress. The barest brush of mouth against mouth. It was briefer than a single heartbeat, yet Susan felt the contact clear down to her toenails. Her eyelids fluttered shut.

"Oh . . ." she began.

". . . yes," he finished.

Kyle's lips sampled hers more deeply. She responded to his slow, sensual savoring. She discovered his tastes and textures at the same time he learned hers.

After a few heady moments, she felt the coaxing glide of his tongue. She opened to him. An instant later, he delved deep into the sweetness of her mouth. She met and matched his sensuous explorations.

The hand cupping her chin slid back, fingers threading deep in her hair. The hand fisted, fingers closing. Even before she felt the gentle tugging on her scalp, Susan was angling her face upward.

The intimacy of the kiss increased. Susan's fingers flexed against Kyle's chest when he caught her lower lip between his teeth, biting down on the acutely sensitive flesh with exquisitely calibrated pressure. She quivered, shaken by a quicksilver burst of sensation radiating from her core.

Kyle circled her waist with his left arm, drawing her close. Susan shifted her hips in an instinctive movement and felt him shudder. His hold on her tightened. The hard ridge of his arousal pulsed against her.

Tongue teasing tongue. Tempting. Tantalizing.

Lips joining lips. Moving in leisurely and languid counterpoint at first. Then merging in fiercer, more fevered acts of courtship and claiming.

Susan was trembling from the depths of her being when the kiss finally came to an end. She made an involuntary sound of protest when Kyle lifted his mouth from hers. Her body arched in frustration as he eased back and away.

They stood there staring at each other for what seemed like forever. Susan had the sense that Kyle was just as stunned as she was. Maybe more so. He, after all, had far more experience by which to gauge the implications of what had just happened between them.

"K-Kyle?" Susan was surprised she could get the word out.

He shook his head. She couldn't tell whether he was warning her against questions or trying to clear his brain. A moment later, he lifted his right hand and touched the tip of his index finger to her lips.

"I've wanted to do that for a long time, Susan," he murmured. "For a long, long time."

There was no doubt that he wanted to do it again. And for a second or two, Susan was absolutely positive he was going to.

But he didn't.

What he *did* do—incredibly—was leave her.

Two nights later, he returned. He returned…and he brought ice cream.

Seven

—

It was 11:43 p.m. Susan was sitting in her son's room, toying with his Bliss Ball and trying to contend with two very different cravings.

The first and more powerful of them centered on Kyle Lochner Gordon, the man she'd heard from just once—a brief, stilted phone call—in the forty-eight hours since he'd kissed her half-senseless and left her standing at her front door. The craving he'd inspired had driven her from her bed approximately forty-five minutes earlier.

The second craving was for mint-chocolate-chip ice cream. At the moment, that was what was urging her to get dressed and go out for a quick fix from the local all-night market.

Susan sighed restlessly and gazed down at the silver sphere cradled in her lap. She ran her fingertips over its softly gleaming curves.

Kyle...

... and mint-chocolate-chip ice cream.

They'd become inexplicably, and inextricably, linked in her mind.

She'd crawled into bed about ten, hoping to catch up on the sleep that had eluded her the previous night. It had been a futile hope. She'd spent an infuriating hour tossing, turning and trying not to think about Kyle before finally admitting defeat. Muttering darkly, she'd switched on the lamp sitting on the nightstand next to the bed, freed herself from the tangle of sheets her thrashing around had created and gotten up.

She'd initially sought to distract herself by going into the living room to watch television. Unfortunately nothing on the tube had been compelling enough to compete with her memories of the man who'd embraced her so passionately, then abandoned her so precipitously two evenings before.

Angered and more than a little aroused by her recollections, she'd turned off the TV and contemplated the other activities open to her. After mentally debating the merits of everything from balancing her checkbook to taking a freezing cold shower, she'd settled on the idea of starting the cleaning job she'd vowed to do while her son was away at science camp. As she'd stalked down the hall, she'd assured herself that the challenge of dealing with the mess in Charlie's room would absorb all her attention.

It was impossible for Susan to say precisely when, or exactly why, her unsettled mood had begun to ease. If she'd been inclined toward fantasy, she would have linked the change in her emotional state to Charlie's Bliss Ball. Never mind that the thing had nearly hit her on the head when it and about a dozen other items had come avalanching down from a shelf the instant she'd opened the door to her son's junk-crammed closet. Within moments of retrieving the silvery globe from the floor, she'd felt a strange sense of serenity settle over her.

She'd found herself curiously reluctant to put the Bliss Ball aside once she'd started touching it. Charlie's artless comment about how the sphere "felt good" had come back to her as she'd stroked its voluptuously smooth surface. There was something profoundly... pleasing about the metal object.

Maybe it was the way the globe seemed to warm to her handling, as though it relished the physical contact.

Maybe it was the way it seemed to shimmer and shift colors, as though it was trying to retain her attention.

Then again, maybe sleep deprivation and sexual frustration were prompting her to imagine that a perfectly ordinary piece of junk was an otherworldly treasure endowed with incredible powers.

Whatever the case, there was no denying that holding the Bliss Ball had had a very soothing effect on her. Nor was there any denying that one of her responses to this soothing effect had been to develop a craving for mint-chocolate-chip ice cream.

That she'd succumbed to an attack of the midnight munchies wasn't surprising. She'd had almost no appetite for food during the previous two days. But to fixate on mint-chocolate-chip ice cream? *That* was peculiar. No matter that mint-chocolate-chip ice cream had been her favorite treat during childhood. She hadn't tasted the stuff, hadn't even been tempted by it, in years!

Susan ran her tongue slowly over her lips. She could taste it now, she realized. She could taste the flavor of mint-chocolate-chip ice cream almost as vividly as she could taste the uniquely male essence of Kyle Gordon's kiss.

She squeezed the Bliss Ball, shockingly conscious of the sudden peaking of her nipples against the oversize cotton T-shirt she wore to sleep in. She felt a knot of need clench like a fist deep within her body. Shifting her position, she pressed her thighs together in a convulsive movement. There was a throb of response. The knot relaxed for a single melting instant, then re-formed, tighter than before.

She wanted him. She wanted Kyle so much she ached with it. And she knew in her heart of hearts that if she looked out the window right now and saw him pull up in front of her house in his gas-guzzling, raging-red Thunderbird she'd run to the door and—

That's when she heard it.

Susan froze, unable to speak, scarcely able to breathe. Her hold on the Bliss Ball slackened. The silvery globe rolled off her lap and bounced across the floor, finally disappearing under Charlie's bed.

She didn't need to look out the window to know who had just pulled up in front of her house in what. All she had to do was listen. The sounds that heralded Kyle's arrival in his classic crimson T-bird were impossible to mistake—or ignore.

I've lost my mind, Kyle decided as he brought his car to a halt and killed the engine. That's the only rational explanation for this. I've done a U-turn on the highway of life and I'm heading into the Twilight Zone.

The notion was not a new one. The possibility that he might be succumbing to some form of insanity had been nagging at the edges of his consciousness for the past forty-eight hours. Still, it seemed to him that certain elements of his present behavior elevated possibility to probability—maybe even flat-out certainty.

Gripping the T-bird's steering wheel, Kyle stared at the exterior of Susan's house. There was an unfamiliar sedan in the driveway. He experienced several knife-edged seconds of anxiety before realizing it must be the loaner Susan was using while her station wagon was in for repairs. He recalled she'd mentioned something about it during the very careful telephone conversation they'd had the morning after their date.

After a moment or two, Kyle started to wonder why there were so many lights on inside the Brookses' house. It was almost midnight, for heaven's sake! A lamp shining in Susan's bedroom he could understand. But why were lights on in the living room? And why in the corner room he knew to be Charlie's? What was going on that required so much illumination?

Why don't you get off your butt, go up and knock on the door and find out? the voice inside his skull suggested with a touch of asperity. *Susan's obviously home. She's obviously awake. Maybe she's been having the same kind of trouble sleeping as you.*

Kyle caught his breath, startled by the unexpected kibitzing. His inner voice had had remarkably little to say during the past few weeks. Aside from an occasional raspberry from his cerebral peanut gallery, he'd pretty much been left to police his own actions and attitudes. The weird thing was he was turning out to be more demanding of himself than the voice had ever been.

How do I explain my coming over here at this time of night? he countered, continuing to eye the brightly lit house. What if something's wrong? Really wrong?

No, he decided almost immediately. He'd know if there was something wrong. He didn't know how he'd know; he just knew he would.

Ever heard of telling the truth? the voice queried.

Oh, sure. Right. I'm supposed to tell Susan that after two days of staying away from her, I was overwhelmed by a sudden need to drive over and visit?

A sudden need? You call something that's been eating at you for years a sudden *need?*

Kyle shifted his position abruptly, dimly registering the restraint of his seat belt. The voice was right, of course. There was nothing sudden about his wanting to be near Susan. His yearning for her—the yearning he'd tried to deny into dormancy for so long—was more than a decade old.

He wanted her. He wanted her so much it frightened him. He didn't know how to deal with the desires she evoked or the dreams she inspired. They were outside the realm of his experience.

The first and only kiss he and Susan had shared had been outside the realm of his experience, too. Nothing in his life— not even the exhilaration of flying—had prepared him for the impact of that caress. He'd stumbled away from it in a state of shock, his senses reeling.

Kyle shifted his body again, acutely aware of the press of his manhood against the front of his tightly zippered jeans. Hunger prowled through his bloodstream like a barely leashed predator, sharpening its claws, showing its teeth and straining the limits of his self-discipline.

But what do I have to offer her? he demanded silently. The question was one he'd asked himself more times than he cared to count during the past two days. His inability to provide a satisfactory answer to it was the primary reason he'd limited his post-kiss contact with Susan to a single telephone call.

Well, there's that quart of mint-chocolate-chip ice cream you insisted on picking up, came the acerbic reply.

Kyle glanced at the brown paper bag sitting to his right. Its contents, more than anything else, seemed to underscore his shaky grip on sanity. Giving in to an urge to drive over to Susan's house in the middle of the night made sense in a crazy kind of way. But feeling compelled to stop en route to purchase a quart of ice cream . . .

That was lunacy. Sheer unadulterated lunacy!

And there was more. The impulse behind his ice-cream buying had been an extremely specific one. He'd known when he'd pulled into the parking lot of the local twenty-four-hour convenience store that no flavor but mint-chocolate-chip would serve his purpose—whatever the hell that purpose was intended to be.

Great, Kyle thought, turning his gaze back to the house. I can offer the lady a late-night snack.

Just part of being one of the best times around, hot dog.

Kyle went rigid. Susan deserves a damned sight more than a good time from me!

Did you ever stop to consider that might be all she wants—or needs—right now?

What's that supposed to mean?

She kissed you Friday night, didn't she? You didn't force it. You didn't fantasize it. You kissed her and she kissed you back.

Yes, but—

Do you think she's ever kissed Jack Wiley like that?

I *know* she never kissed Jack Wiley like that.

Fine. What about Mike? Do you think she ever kissed him the way she kissed you?

Kyle's throat closed up. His chest went tight, as though banded with straps of steel.

He'd never allowed himself to speculate about Susan's physical relationship with Mike. From the very beginning, at the most basic of levels, he'd always considered that particular subject utterly off-limits and absolutely taboo.

No matter that he'd known his best friend had gone to the altar with less sexual experience than he, himself, had had at age seventeen. No matter that he'd strongly suspected his best friend's bride had been equally innocent when she'd glided up the aisle in her white lace and orange blossoms. No matter that he hadn't sensed the slightest crackle of electricity between the two when they'd exchanged their first embrace as husband and wife.

He simply hadn't permitted himself to think about Susan and Mike. Alone. Together. As woman and man.

Never, ever.

Kyle swallowed hard. He sucked in a breath, like a drowning man struggling to survive.

He wasn't going to start thinking about it now, either, he told himself fiercely. Susan and Mike were in the past. Susan and he were . . . were . . .

"What?" Kyle asked aloud. "What are we?"

The warm summer night was silent. And so, for nearly a minute, was the voice inside his skull. Then:

It's right for you to be here. Can't you feel that?

Dammit, I don't know what I feel!

Yes, you do. You know you do. Stop running away from it.

Kyle looked toward the house once again. He saw a movement at the window of Charlie's bedroom. Susan, he thought instantly. Need boiled up within him, like water from a volcanic spring.

After a moment, he moved his right hand from the steering wheel to his seat belt. It took him three fumbling tries to release the buckle.

What if she says no?

It won't kill you.

Kyle retrieved the ice cream, then reached for the door handle. What if she says . . . yes?

That won't kill you, either. But even if it did, it'd be a hell of a way to go. Like flying.

Kyle felt himself smile. The curve that reshaped his mouth was sudden and very, very certain. If it wasn't the Gordon Grin, it was close.

No, he amended. Better.

The clock on the kitchen wall read 12:21 a.m. The second of Susan Eleanor Brooks's cravings had been thoroughly satisfied. As for the first . . .

"More?" Kyle questioned, indicating the container of ice cream sitting to his left.

"No, thank you," Susan refused, dropping her spoon into the bowl she knew she'd emptied with embarrassing speed. She realized that jittery nerves had been just as responsible as genuine hunger for the haste of her consumption.

"Are you sure? There's plenty left."

She shook her head, eyeing the barely touched contents of the dish in front of her companion. "You don't like mint-chocolate-chip ice cream?"

"Actually, I'm more a maple-walnut kind of guy."

"Then why...?"

"I told you when you let me in. I got this crazy urge to bring you mint-chocolate-chip ice cream and I gave in to it."

Susan twiddled with the belt of the knee-length terry-cloth robe she'd donned before she'd dashed to answer Kyle's ringing summons. She was acutely aware of the way she must look. Bare feet. Naked face. Finger-fluffed hair. Why, oh why, had she been in such a rush? she asked herself. Had she honestly believed that Kyle would turn away and leave if she didn't fling the front door open two seconds after he pressed the bell?

Maybe she had.

Maybe she hadn't.

The bottom line was, she hadn't wanted to take the risk. Hence, her unslippered feet, unmade-up face and uncombed hair.

Two nights before, Kyle had told her she was beautiful and made her believe it. She wondered fleetingly how drastically he'd revised that opinion during the past half hour.

"Does this sort of thing happen very often?" she queried after a few moments.

Kyle arched a tawny brow. "What sort of thing? My getting crazy urges? Or my giving in to them?"

"Either." She shifted, conscious of the nubby texture of the terry cloth as it rubbed against her upper thighs. Her skin suddenly seemed unusually sensitive. "Both."

Kyle shrugged. The easy movement made the sleek muscles of his broad shoulders ripple against the fabric of his black cotton T-shirt. Then he smiled. The lazy curling of his sensual lips brought both his dimples briefly into play.

Susan knew there'd been a time when she would have accepted the offhandedness of these two nonverbal responses at face value. But that time was over and gone. She sought the answers she needed in Kyle's brilliant blue eyes. The expression she saw in them was anything but casual. Whatever was going on—and there was no doubt in her mind that whatever it was it was desperately important—the man sitting across the kitchen table from her was as caught up in it as she was.

"Kyle?" she prompted after several long seconds of silence.

The smile vanished. The lean, powerful body went still. "Yes and no."

She blinked, confused. "I don't—"

"Yes, I've gotten crazy urges. And yes, I've given in to them. But no, not very often. And no—" Kyle leaned forward very suddenly, his eyes locking with hers "—never like tonight, Susan. Never, ever."

Susan sustained his gaze as long as she could. It wasn't very long. Looking down, she began twiddling with the belt of her robe again. Her fingers were unsteady. So was her voice when she finally mustered sufficient breath to speak.

"In...in other words..." She paused, swallowing hard. "You haven't made a practice of, uh, showing up at women's houses at midnight with cartons of ice cream."

Kyle made a sound that might have been a laugh. Then he said, "This is my first time."

The response brought her head back up. She could feel her cheeks start to heat. "Why mint-chocolate-chip?"

"Why not?"

"It's my favorite flavor, Kyle," she answered, stressing a point she'd made earlier.

He sat back, his expression shuttered, his body language wary. Susan had the sense that something about the singular appropriateness of his ice-cream selection had shaken him deeply. "I told you your opinion matters to me, Susan."

"But how could you know my opinion about ice cream? I've never mentioned it."

Kyle averted his gaze. Susan saw his jaw clench. There was tension in every line of his neck and shoulders. "I had a feeling," he answered. "Just . . . a feeling, all right? I can't explain it." He grimaced, then added with obvious reluctance, "That seems to be turning into a chronic problem for me."

"What? Having feelings?"

"Not being able to explain them."

"Have you tried?"

He faced her once again, his eyes challenging. "Do you want me to?"

Susan cocked her chin. "That depends."

"On what?"

The memory of the serenity she'd experienced earlier gave Susan the courage to answer without coyness. "On whether these feelings you say you can't explain have anything to do with me."

Frankness begat frankness and then some.

"They have everything to do with you." Kyle's tone was identical to the one he'd used a little more than two weeks ago when he'd told her he didn't know why her opinion was so important to him, only that it was.

There was a pause. Then Susan broached the question that had been gnawing at her peace of mind for most of the previous forty-eight hours.

"Are these . . . feelings the reason you walked away from me Friday night?"

"I didn't walk away from you."

The statement was quick and unequivocal and, from Susan's point of view, completely untrue.

"No?" she countered, drawing herself up. "Well, then, how would you describe what you did, Kyle? I mean, one minute we were kissing and the next minute—"

"I was running scared."

Susan's breath jammed at the top of her throat like a cork. "What?" she eventually managed to force out.

Kyle repeated his words.

"Are you saying you were afraid?" Of all the possible explanations for his behavior she'd come up with . . .

Afraid? Kyle Gordon? No, she thought.

"Yes," he said.

"Of . . . of what?"

"Of pushing too far, too fast. Of taking too much and giving too little. Of getting things wrong I wanted to get absolutely right." Kyle raked his right hand back through his hair. The abruptness of the gesture hinted at a wealth of pent-up emotion. "Of hearing you tell me to . . . stop."

Susan shifted, trying to absorb the implications of Kyle's extraordinary admission. Her mind could barely take in the words, much less assign them weight and meaning.

"And now?" she finally asked.

Kyle's gaze never wavered from hers. "I'm still afraid, Susan."

"But—" she gestured " —you're here."

Kyle shoved his chair back and got to his feet in a seamless movement. For one awful instant, Susan thought he was going to leave her once again. She opened her mouth to protest. The words died on her lips as she recognized his true intention.

Her pulse stammered, steadied, then speeded up. She felt herself start to tremble.

Kyle walked noiselessly around to where she was sitting. He stood, gazing down at her. Watching. Waiting. His features were rigidly set, his breathing unnaturally steady.

Susan pushed her chair away from the kitchen table. Slowly. Very slowly. After a moment, she stood up. A tiny portion of her mind registered surprise that her legs were capable of supporting her. She could have sworn that every bone in her body had turned to jelly.

She reached out to touch Kyle. She had to. He intercepted her hand and raised it to his mouth, brushing the knuckles of her fingers with his lips. The feather-light contact sent an electric tingle skittering up her arm.

"There are feelings stronger than fear," he said huskily. His eyes flickered like twin sapphire flames. "Feelings like need . . . and want . . ."

Need. Want. The sound of these two one-syllable words triggered a lightning flash of disappointment in Susan. It lasted less than an instant, yet it illuminated her own unacknowl-edged feelings so vividly she nearly cried out in shock.

She'd fallen in love with him. Dear God. *She'd fallen in love with Kyle Gordon!*

"Susan?" he asked, releasing her hand.

Dazed by the momentous discovery she'd just made about herself, Susan looked up. She wasn't certain whether her world was coming together or falling apart. The only thing she was sure of was that whatever was happening, Kyle Lochner Gordon was at the epicenter of it.

"You . . . want me?" she said in a voice that sounded noth-ing like her own.

For a moment, Kyle seemed to stop breathing. His face tightened, his angular features acquiring a peculiar kind of clarity that made him look both older and younger than his years.

"More than anything on Earth," was all he said.

Susan hesitated for the space of a single heartbeat before making her decision. She went up on tiptoe, lifting her arms and circling his neck. "I want you, too," she told the man she loved.

And then she kissed him.

Kyle was no novice when it came to women's boudoirs or what men were expected to do in them. Yet sometime between the moment he lifted Susan into his arms in her cozy kitchen and the moment he crossed the threshold into her peach-and-cream bedroom, he realized that he'd committed himself to a new kind of experience. What he'd done in the past no longer seemed to apply. The present, so bright, so burning, was all that mattered.

He heard Susan make a throaty little sound as he set her down on her feet just a few steps away from her unmade bed. Her arms were still twined around his neck, her mouth still pressed against his.

"Susan," he murmured, nibbling and nuzzling her lips. "Oh, sweet . . . oh, Susan . . ."

He wanted to explore every fresh and feminine inch of her body. To discover all her secrets. To learn her wildest fantasies

and to make them come true. Kyle wanted to know Susan as
well as he knew himself. No. He wanted to know her better than
that. Much better.

"Kyle," she whispered, moving against him in sensual sup-
plication. "Oh . . . yes."

He'd resented the terry-cloth robe Susan was wearing from
the first second he'd seen it. Compared to the lovely vulnerability of the rest of her appearance, its barrierlike bulk had
seemed like a reproach. The chance to rid her of the garment
came, and he took it, easing the robe off her shoulders and
down her arms, then tossing it carelessly aside.

He caressed her from throat to thigh in slow, sweeping
strokes, savoring the warm resilience of her flesh through the
cotton of her loose-fitting T-shirt. He cupped the ripe, rounded
weight of her breasts, feathering his thumbs against the thin
fabric that did nothing to disguise their peaking crests. She
gasped, her breath seeming to shatter somewhere between her
lungs and lips. The soft, broken sound was intoxicating to Kyle.
He covered her mouth with his own once again, savoring the
hot honeyed taste of her response.

After a few heady moments, he felt Susan's hands slide from
his shoulders to his waist. She began to pull at the fabric of his
T-shirt.

Two tugs. The first tentative, the second anything but.

The garment was pulled free of his jeans. A second later Susan was touching his naked skin. Her palms were soft, her fingers splayed and searching. She defined the shape of his upper
body like a sculptor, exploring every line and sinew with exquisitely erotic care.

And then it was Kyle's turn to gasp. He spoke Susan's name
on a shuddery inhalation as she found the tightly furled buttons of his nipples. She traced them with teasing fingers, then
raked them lightly with her nails. A white-hot arrow of pleasure streaked down his body. The already taut muscles of his
belly contracted.

Gravity shifted. The throbbing heaviness between his thighs
increased. His wash-faded jeans, already uncomfortably snug,
seemed to shrink two sizes.

More kisses.

More caresses.

Kyle's T-shirt went the way of Susan's terry-cloth bathrobe.

Her top followed a few fevered seconds later. She stood, quivering, clad in nothing but a pristine pair of white cotton panties.

"Susan," Kyle breathed, drinking in the womanly revelations of her nearly naked body.

He'd dreamed of seeing her this way, of course. He'd dreamed of it many times over the course of many years. But not one of those dreams had come close to matching the reality now offered to him.

He laid his hands on her newly bared flesh with something close to reverence, luxuriating in the silken texture of her creamy skin. He charted the shadowed hollow at the base of her slender throat with the balls of his thumbs, then cherished the curving lines of her shoulders and breasts. She flushed wildly as he let his fingers linger on her nipples. He felt a primitive stab of satisfaction as he watched the pink satin peaks tighten into dusky rosettes.

"Kyle. Oh...oh...K-Kyle..." There was both plea and permission in her shaky invocation of his name.

He gathered her to him once again. She turned her face up. He brought his mouth down. Their lips met in passionate fusion. Coaxing. Questing. Clinging. Their breaths mingled. Their tongues mated in a rhythmic evocation of an even more intimate joining.

Kyle deepened the kiss, searching hungrily for the sweetness he'd tasted before. Susan yielded with a purring sigh, her hands flowing up his spine. Her fingers massaged the back of his neck for a moment, then threaded possessively into his hair.

It was not enough for him to take. It was not even sufficient for him to match her unstinting generosity. Kyle wanted to give back every pleasure he was granted in triple measure. He attuned his senses to Susan's needs, holding his own clamoring appetite in check in order to satisfy hers.

To hear her cry out, deep in her throat... To feel her quiver as though responding from her very core...

They moved to the bed. Still kissing. Still caressing. He eased her down and then started to step back. He went rigid when

Susan reached out and caught him by the waistband of his jeans. She stroked him through the denim fabric, seemingly fascinated by the taut bulge of his masculine arousal. After several mind-blowing moments, she began to undo the snap at the top of his fly.

She was like a torch. He was like bone-dry tinder. He groaned, fearing he might go up in flames right then and there. He captured her hands with his own.

"Susan, in the name of heaven . . ." he gasped.

She looked up at him, her tumbled hair shifting back from her face. Her lips were sheened with moisture and slightly parted. Her long-lashed eyes were wide and very dark.

If he hadn't been teetering on the brink already, the open yearning in Susan's expression would have brought him to that perilous state in less than an instant. Kyle felt the bonds of his self-control fraying, second by second, strand by strand.

"Wait," he told her hoarsely. "Sweetheart . . . we have all the time in the world."

"All the time in the world . . . is too long, Kyle," she answered, her voice as unsteady as his breathing. *"Please . . ."*

A dead man might have withstood the plea. Kyle Lochner Gordon, who was very much alive, could not.

Weeks before, she'd accused him of carelessness. He'd long since acknowledged the validity of her charge. But there was one area where he'd never been careless.

He reached around to the back pocket of his jeans. He saw Susan's confusion when he took out his wallet. He saw her confusion give way to startled comprehension when he opened the wallet and extracted a small foil packet.

"I . . . didn't even think . . ." she stammered, her cheeks going crimson. She brought her arms up, crossing them in front of her breasts.

Kyle didn't want her shy or shocked, and he certainly didn't want her ashamed. "Don't," he said quietly. "It's all right, Susan. I'll keep you safe."

It was a pledge he knew he'd do anything to honor. The precautions he'd taken in the past had been rooted in selfishness. No short-term pleasure had ever been worth a long-term price. This was different. This was *Susan* he was protecting.

He unsnapped. Unzipped. Then shucked both his jeans and the briefs beneath.

A few moments later, he and Susan were together on her bed. A few moments after that, she was totally naked.

He tried to tell her with words how often he'd thought of her, how desperately he wanted her. But the challenge of articulating something so all consuming was too great. He let his body communicate his message—caressing her with his eyes, courting her with his mouth and claiming her with his hands.

He stroked the smoothness of her stomach, the gentle swell of her hips, the sweet curves of her bottom. She reciprocated with caresses that ranged from delicate to demanding. He pleasured her with teeth and tongue. She repaid him in kind.

His breath, which had been sawing in and out between his lips, wedged at the top of his throat when he felt her fingers close around him. In the same instant, he pressed his palm against the delta-shaped cluster of dark curls at the juncture of her parted thighs. She arched into the curve of his hand.

He explored the secrets of her petaled femininity, the skin of his fingertips becoming slick with the dew of her arousal. She twisted, arching up once again and crying out her need.

"Kyle . . . oh, Kyle . . ."

There was no way to deny her. No way to delay the inevitable from happening. Kyle moved up and over, then sheathed himself inside Susan with a potent thrust. The fit of their bodies was searingly, shockingly sweet. Far beyond any fantasy.

He heard her inhale on a fragmented series of gasps. He felt the bite of her nails into his shoulders. She rocked her pelvis in an indescribably voluptuous movement, taking him even deeper within herself.

"So . . . beautiful . . ."

"Yes . . . yes . . ."

Somehow, he found the strength to hold back until he sensed the rippling contractions that signaled the beginning of his new lover's release. He went very still, wanting to prolong the moment, to be certain, absolutely certain, of Susan's pleasure.

"Kyle!" she cried out. "Oh . . . please . . ."

Time shattered into a million shimmering pieces. The world spun out of control.

Kyle Lochner Gordon soared toward a star-filled universe of undiscovered, incandescent ecstasy. What he found there, he did not find alone.

Eight

When Susan awoke late the next morning, she was alone in her bed but not in her home. The sounds of a man going about his business in the master bathroom, which had been her exclusive domain for more than two years, assured her of that.

It was an acutely intimate experience—lying amid sheets redolent with the musky aftermath of passion, listening to the lover who, in a single ecstatic night, had irrevocably altered her fundamental perceptions about her own nature. For a few moments, Susan allowed herself to imagine what it would be like to enjoy such intimacy on a daily basis.

She knew her fantasizing was foolish at best, downright dangerous at worst. But she couldn't prevent herself from dreaming. The idea of building a life with the man whose meaning to her she was just beginning to comprehend was too alluring not to be explored.

Susan closed her eyes. Longing sliced into her like a knife, cutting straight to the center of her soul. She felt the tips of her breasts tighten into yearning peaks. She caught her breath, then exhaled on a drawn-out sigh.

How long? she wondered. How long had she been in love with Kyle Gordon? Had it been years? Or only a matter of days?

He'd desired her body and she'd surrendered it to him. Completely. Without inhibition. It was an action she'd taken in full awareness—she was a grown woman, after all, not some innocent girl who'd succumbed to seduction—and she did not have the least regret.

As for the yielding of her heart, which every instinct she possessed told her Kyle had never wanted and never even contemplated happening...

No, she told herself. The love she felt for Kyle was not to be regretted, either.

Even so, she knew she could never speak of this love. She knew she could never show it more explicitly than she already had. Nor could she use her emotions to try to bind her lover of one night into a permanent partner. When Kyle left—as she had no doubt he ultimately would—she'd kiss him goodbye, wish him Godspeed and let him go.

She cared for him too deeply to do any less. Or any more.

Susan opened her eyes abruptly. She sat up, clutching the sheets around her body. Her pulse kicked as she heard the sound of a toilet being flushed. A second or two later, the man she had fallen in love with appeared in the doorway between her bedroom and the master bath.

For the first few moments, all she could do was stare at him.

She found herself registering odd fragments of his appearance. The strands of damp hair that refused to be sleeked back from his brow. The razor nick on his chin. The undone snap on the waistband of his low-riding jeans.

She recalled—very vividly—how she had reached for that small metal fastener the night before. She'd been feverishly eager to touch Kyle, and she'd resented anything that lay between her hands and his body.

The memory of her boldness made Susan tighten her grip on the sheets. After a brief hesitation, she forced herself to meet Kyle's gaze.

"Good morning," he said.

Susan's first impression was of emotional distance bordering on indifference. Then she noticed the coiled-spring tension in his posture and began to revise her assessment.

His breathing was just a tad too steady.... His features were just a tad too carefully schooled....

He's nervous, she concluded with a shock. He's as nervous as I am!

"Good morning," she returned after a moment, wishing her voice sounded a little less breathy.

"Are you—" a pause, as though he was hunting for precisely the right words "—all right?"

Susan shifted, unnervingly conscious of the intensity of Kyle's gaze. "I'm fine. And you?"

He lifted his right hand and rubbed his palm against his chest. The action made the well-toned muscles of his torso ripple. Susan's fingers tingled with a desire to chart the subtle movements.

"I'm fine, too," he said.

There was a short silence. During the course of it, Susan was forced to acknowledge that she'd been depending on Kyle to guide her through the inevitable complexities of this morning-after-the-night-before encounter. Although she didn't consider herself naive, she was aware that her grasp of contemporary sexual etiquette was limited.

Witness, for example, her response to the condom Kyle had produced so matter-of-factly the night before. At first she'd been shocked. Not that he'd been prepared to take precautions, but that she hadn't even considered the fact that they were necessary. Once the shock had receded she'd found herself thinking about the implications of his readiness to assume responsibility for protecting her and himself.

"I'll keep you safe," he'd told her...and she'd believed him. She still believed him.

Susan shifted again, readjusting her hold on the sheets. Kyle didn't budge from the doorway.

"Have you been up long?" she asked.

He shrugged. "Awhile."

"You should have woken me."

A smile—half rueful, half reminiscent—ghosted around the corners of Kyle's mouth. Susan's heart performed a sudden hop-skip-jump. He'd watched her, she realized. He'd watched her while she'd lain beside him, sleeping. An odd thrill of pleasure skittered up her spine.

"You were pretty much out of it, Susan." The bluntness of Kyle's words was at odds with the slow curving of his lips. "I thought you could use the rest."

Susan swallowed, shifting her position for a third time. She glanced around her pastel-painted bedroom, cataloging a setting that seemed both comfortingly familiar and indescribably strange. Her gaze glided over the fuchsia teddy bear that had been ensconced on top of her bureau for nearly a month, then slipped to the floor. The clothes she'd been wearing the night before were lying on a pale kilim rug by the bed.

Trying to quell the voluptuous memory of how those clothes had come to be where they were, she looked back at Kyle. "I, ah, haven't been sleeping very well lately," she admitted awkwardly.

He laughed humorlessly. "Tell me about it."

"You've been having trouble sleeping, too?"

The expression in his eyes was very frank. "Oh, yeah."

There was another silence, somewhat longer than the previous one. Eventually Kyle crossed from the bathroom doorway to the left side of Susan's bed. He stood for a moment or two, as though waiting for an invitation or an objection, then slowly seated himself on the edge of the mattress.

"I borrowed a razor," he said, indicating the small cut on his chin. "I hope you don't mind."

"Not at all," she assured him sincerely. "Feel free to make yourself at home."

The last sentence just slipped out. Susan saw Kyle stiffen in apparent response to it. She wanted to bite her tongue.

Feel free to make yourself at home.

Lord! Even if she hadn't meant the remark the way he'd obviously taken it—and given her feelings, she couldn't deny the possibility that she had—it had been an idiotic thing for her to say.

"Kyle, I—"

"Susan, I—"

They spoke in unison, with a similar degree of urgency. They both stopped speaking at precisely the same instant.

"You go first," Susan said after a few seconds.

Kyle shook his head. "No. You."

Susan hesitated, moistening suddenly dry lips with a quick dart of her tongue. She saw a flame spark to life deep in Kyle's brilliant blue eyes.

Want, she told herself. Want and need.

Not love.

Kyle had been open about the nature of his feelings for her the night before. He hadn't tried to disguise his desires with flowery words or false promises. He'd been absolutely honest.

She, on the other hand, had hidden the truth about her emotions. She'd lied by a deliberate act of omission. And there was no retreating from what she'd done. She couldn't tell Kyle the truth. She had to continue as she'd begun. She had no choice.

"I don't want you to think I'm making...assumptions," she said finally.

"Assumptions?"

"I know how what I said a minute ago, about making yourself at home, probably sounded to you. But it wasn't..." She gestured with one hand. "I'm not expecting more, Kyle. I understand what last night was."

His eyes narrowed. "And what was it, Susan?"

She shifted yet again. "We made love together. And it was wonderful."

"But?" The word was edged.

She shook her head, feeling herself flush. Why was he making this so difficult? she asked herself with a touch of anger.

"No buts," she answered. Her mind flashed back to the explanation he'd offered about Jenna Bradley three days before. "And no strings attached."

His face went blank. Trying to get a fix on what he was feeling behind the blankness—and Susan was positive he must be feeling something—was like trying to claw a path up a polished glass wall.

Finally he spoke. His voice was a few notes lower than usual. "In other words, we had a good time, let's leave it at that."

For one insane instant, Susan had the impression he was hurt. A wild sense of hope welled up inside her. Sweet heaven, was it possible Kyle didn't want to "leave it at that"? Was it possible he—

Stop it! she ordered herself. Just . . . *stop* it!

Kyle reached out and touched her then, stroking the side of her face with his knuckles. Susan turned her cheek into the caress.

After a few seconds, he resumed speaking. "You know, when I think back to the first time I ever saw you, I—"

Susan forestalled whatever he was going to say by the simple expedient of pressing her fingers to his lips. She didn't want to hear his version of their first meeting. Not now. Not ever.

"The first time you saw me I was a twenty-one-year-old girl who believed she was going to live happily ever after," she said. "That girl is gone, Kyle. The orange blossoms she was wearing have wilted, and the white-lace gown she had on probably doesn't fit anymore. I'm a thirty-two-year-old widow with a ten-year-old son. I . . . I'm also a woman with wants."

"And you want me." All hint of the hurt Susan had thought she'd detected less than a minute before was gone. She had the feeling Kyle had come to some kind of decision.

"I told you I did last night." She knew she'd tell him the same thing now if he asked. It would be the truth, as far as it went.

The hand that had been stroking her cheek drifted slowly down her throat and curved to fit the naked line of her right shoulder. After a moment, Kyle lifted his right hand and cupped her other shoulder.

"I can't offer you any promises about how long I'm going to stay in Wilder's Forge, Susan," he said quietly, buffing the ridge of her collarbone.

"I know that." She swallowed. "But . . . you will be here until Charlie gets back from camp, won't you?"

Kyle slid his hands inward until his thumbs touched. They met less than an inch above the start of the cleft between her breasts. "That's twelve days from now."

"Yes." Susan inhaled shakily, conscious that the sheet she'd been clutching so modestly was slipping downward. She felt her nipples pucker.

"Not very long." He began to draw her toward him. Slowly. Very, very slowly. As though he wanted to grant her every possible opportunity to call a halt to what was happening.

Stopping him—or herself—was the last thing Susan wanted to do.

"We can make it seem...like all...the time...in the world," she whispered, paraphrasing something he'd told her the night before.

She saw Kyle's eyes blaze and knew he'd recognized her words as his own. "We can damned well try," he declared fiercely, then gathered her into his arms.

She turned her face up for his kiss. The man she loved took everything she offered and gave her far more than she asked.

"Is something wrong, Susan?" Kyle asked two nights later. They were lingering over coffee at the same restaurant they'd patronized the evening of their first kiss.

"Wrong?"

"You seem . . . distracted."

Susan hesitated for a moment. "I was thinking about Charlie."

"Oh?" He'd been thinking about her son, too. He'd been debating whether he should reveal the contents of a letter he'd received from Charlie that afternoon.

"I got a letter from him today," she said.

Kyle traced the rim of his coffee cup. "Trouble?"

A hint of ruefulness crimped her lips. "I'm not sure."

"Do you have the letter with you?"

"In my purse."

"Why don't you read it to me?"

"All right."

The white envelope Susan removed from her purse was identical to the one he'd found in his uncle's mailbox roughly six hours earlier. The blue-lined sheet of paper she took out was the twin of the one he had tucked away in the inner pocket of the blazer he was wearing.

Susan unfolded the paper. "My maternal instincts are probably working overtime," she observed with a little laugh. "But here goes. 'Dear Mom. Hi, from me. Your son, Charlie. At camp.'"

"Sounds promising so far."

"Just wait. 'I am having a great time. All the kids here are really smart. So are the counselors. The weather is fine. The food is good. We had tuna-noodle casserole twice.'" She glanced across the table. "That's casserole spelled with a *k* and two *l*s, by the way."

Kyle chuckled. "He's at science camp, Susan."

"Charlie hates tuna-noodle casserole."

"Well, I'm not particularly fond of it, either."

"You don't think that paragraph sounds suspicious?"

He shook his head. "Actually, I think it sounds...reassuring."

"Too reassuring. He's not telling me everything."

How true, Kyle thought wryly. Charlie, buddy, I think you may have outsmarted yourself on this one.

"Is there more?" he asked.

Susan eyed him for a moment, then returned to the letter. "'I have this new friend named Mark,'" she read. "'He is very interesting. I gave him some of my underwear because he forgot his.'"

Kyle smothered a chuckle. He'd gotten an earful about Charlie's underwear during the drive up to camp.

Susan glanced at him again, then returned to her reading. "'I hope you are okay. Is your car alive again? How is Kyle? Did you—'" she cleared her throat "'—have any more dates with Mr. Wiley? See you. Love, Charlie. P.S. I really want a pet. Can I get one?'"

There was a pause. Susan refolded the letter and slipped it back into the envelope. Then she looked at Kyle. He gazed back, sensing she wasn't buying his composed expression any more than she'd bought her son's carefully contrived correspondence. Her next words confirmed this intuition.

"You've heard from him, haven't you, Kyle?"

He nodded.

"Will you tell me what he said?"

The anxiety in her brown eyes made up his mind for him. He reached inside his jacket. "Better yet, I'll read his letter to you."

"Thank you."

"Hold your gratitude until after you hear it," he advised dryly.

She stiffened. "Is it *that* bad?"

"To another guy, no. To a mom ..."

"Oh, Lord."

Kyle unfolded the letter and began to read. "'Dear Kyle. Hi. This is from me, Charlie. Camp is the most seriously excellent time I've ever had. Yesterday, me and my new friend Mark kind of reinvented gunpowder. There was an explosion. It was pretty awesome.'"

There was a gasp from the other side of the table. Kyle waited a moment, then continued reading. He kept his demeanor as neutral as possible.

"'Don't worry, though. My eyebrows are supposed to grow back before I get home. Oh, yeah. Could you please lend me some money to help pay for the window that broke when the experiment blew up?'"

Susan groaned. Kyle looked over at her. Although she seemed genuinely appalled, he also caught a glint of amusement in her eyes.

"Do you want me to go on?" he asked.

"I don't know." She grimaced. "*Do* I?"

"You're only going to imagine the worst if you don't hear the rest."

"It's not the worst, then?"

"Nowhere near."

She lifted her chin with a feistiness he'd come to relish. "All right," she declared. "I'm braced. Go on."

Kyle complied. "'Today we had a talk from a herpetologist. He told us how to milk rattlesnakes but said we shouldn't try it at home. Tomorrow or the next day a spider expert is coming. He's bringing black widows and tarantulas. Anyway. How are you? How is Mom? Don't tell me if she's going on dates with Mr. Wiley. See you. Your buddy, Charlie.'"

A pause.

"Is that ... all?"

"Well, there *is* a P.S.," Kyle conceded. "It has to do with his wanting to get a pet."

"A rattlesnake," Susan instantly deduced. "He wants you to talk me into letting him have a rattlesnake."

Her tacit acknowledgment of his ability to influence her where her son was concerned surprised Kyle. So did the surge of pleasure he felt at her apparently unconscious admission. "No," he denied after a moment.

"I am *not* going to have black widows and tarantulas in my house."

"Relax, Susan. Charlie wants one pet. Singular."

She sighed, shoulders slumping. "Read the P.S."

"Okay. Ahem. 'P.S. I have a chance to adopt this rat. He's an orphan. What do you think?' "

Susan was as still as a stone for about ten seconds. Then she started laughing. Helplessly. Hilariously. After a moment, Kyle joined in. The lure of her laughter was impossible to resist.

"A r-rat?" she finally repeated, struggling for breath. Her cheeks were flushed. Her eyes were diamond bright. "My son w-wants to adopt a *rat* as a pet?"

"Don't—" Kyle gulped for air "—forget the orphan part."

That set Susan off again. "Oh, no," she spluttered. "Of c-course not."

Eventually she ran out of steam. The laughter faded to throaty chortles, then tailed off into silence. Kyle saw her expression grow pensive. Their gazes touched across the table. He felt a familiar stir of response. Her eyes enticed him with the mystery of infinite, eternal femininity.

"What do *you* think?" she asked. Her voice held a hint of huskiness.

"About Charlie getting a pet?"

She nodded.

"I think we can do a lot better for the kid than an orphan rat."

Susan smiled at him. Kyle wasn't certain why. He only knew that watching the sudden curving of her lips was like watching the sun come out from behind a cloud. It warmed him in ways he'd never been warmed before.

He began to realize there was very little he wouldn't do to be warmed in those ways again.

Kyle had never had much time for envy. He'd always considered it a pretty pointless emotion. Yet eight days after he and Susan became lovers, he found himself envying the oregano-scented tomato sauce Fiori's used on top of its best-selling everything-but-anchovies pizza.

"I wish you'd stop that," he growled, crumpling his paper napkin and tossing it down next to his plate.

Susan paused in the midst of licking the sauce-smeared tips of her fingers. "Stop what?"

As if she didn't know. As if she didn't know he knew she knew. "The X-rated pizza-eating act."

Susan cocked her head, appearing to consider his expression. Then, without shifting her gaze, she removed a spicy-looking slice of pepperoni from the wedge of pizza sitting on the plate in front of her. She lifted the tidbit to her lips and proceeded to eat it in a series of teeny-tiny bites.

Kyle felt his body tighten in reaction to every...single...nibble.

He'd discovered a lot of exciting things about Susan during the past eight days. Among them, her talent for teasing. He was still a long way from determining exactly how far she'd go to provoke the reactions she wanted from him. Then again, he wasn't particularly inclined to resist her provocations.

"I'm afraid I don't know what you're talking about, Kyle," Susan informed him. She selected another piece of pepperoni.

"Keep on the way you're going and you're likely to get a very explicit explanation," he warned.

She lifted her brows. "What, here? In Fiori's?" She shook her head, her dark hair waving softly around her face and over her shoulders. "That's not your style."

"I might surprise you, Susan."

"No. I don't think so." Susan popped the entire piece of pepperoni into her mouth, then chewed and swallowed. "I know all your best tricks."

"Oh, really?"

"Mmm."

"So... I misread your reaction yesterday morning."

Susan picked up her napkin and dabbed delicately at her lips. Her dark eyes were dancing. "My reaction? To what?"

Kyle kept his expression serious, savoring the lovers' game they were playing. He wondered whether Susan would object to his exceeding the speed limit on the drive back to her house. "The bear," he specified.

She batted her lashes at him. "And which bear might that be?"

"The fat fuzzy fuchsia one that sits on your dresser. The one that's almost as pink as you were when I used it to—"

"Oh, *that* bear!" She blushed.

"You weren't surprised, hmm?"

"Well..." She wadded up her napkin and put it down on the table. Kyle was pleased to note that her hands were trembling.

"I could have sworn there was some genuine surprise in that shriek of yours," he drawled.

Susan stiffened, objecting to his choice of words. "Shriek?"

"Yeah. It sounded sort of like—"

"Never mind," she cut him off. "I know what it sounded like."

"It's all coming back to you, right?"

"Kyle—"

"Including your being surprised."

"I wasn't *surprised*," she insisted. "Not really. You caught me... off guard."

He flashed her a wicked, deliberately wolfish grin. "Funny. I seem to remember catching you naked in the shower."

"Kyle!"

He deep-sixed the grin and leaned forward. "That's almost it, Susan," he informed her with mock gravity. "That's almost the shriek."

For a moment or two, Kyle thought he might get smacked with a piece of pizza. He actually figured he had it coming, all things considered. Then Susan started to laugh. "You're incorrigible," she said.

Kyle leaned back in his seat, playing it nonchalant. "Well, I certainly try."

"That poor teddy bear is probably ruined, you realize. Charlie's going to be very upset."

Kyle dismissed this eventuality with a casual gesture. "Don't worry. A good, ah . . . What was it Charlie said Wendy Marino wanted to give me? Oh, yes. A good blower job and the bear will be just fine. Trust me."

Susan laughed again, then expanded on a previous assessment. "Totally incorrigible."

"And you love it."

Brown eyes locked with blue for a single sizzling second. Susan stopped laughing. The bloom of color faded from her cheeks.

Damn, thought Kyle. *Damn, what a stupid thing to say!*

Of course Susan didn't love "it"—or him. And he had absolutely no right to expect that she would. They'd agreed to the limits of this relationship at the very start.

Two consenting adults, enjoying each other. No strings attached. That's what she wanted from him. That's what he wanted from her. And yet—

Stop it, Kyle ordered himself.

If Susan wanted more from you, could you give it? No way. No how. Jenna pegged you right, hot dog. You're the best time around. That's the bottom line. So don't screw up what you've got by looking for something you can't handle. Because what you've got is a hell of a lot more than you ever thought you'd have. And it's a hell of a lot more than you deserve!

"Susan—" he began.

She stopped him with a quick shake of her head. "It's all right, Kyle," she said quietly. "I understand."

He believed her. That should have made him feel better. Somehow . . . it didn't.

Nine

Several blissful hours after she and Kyle arrived back at her home from Fiori's, Susan raised an issue she had been wondering about for days.

"Kyle?" She shifted languidly beneath the rucked-up bed sheets.

"Mm?" He sounded thoroughly sated and half-asleep.

"Has your uncle asked you where you've been spending your nights?"

Kyle chuckled softly. Positioned as she was, with her right cheek resting against his chest, Susan felt the laughter more than she actually heard it. She levered herself up so she could look at his face.

"What's so funny?" she asked, batting a lock of hair off her cheek.

He ran a caressing hand from her shoulder to her hip. "At the moment, H.G. is barely aware I'm alive."

"I don't understand."

He smothered a yawn. "My uncle's writing on deadline."

"You're saying he's very absorbed in what he's doing?"

"I'm saying he's totally oblivious to reality." Kyle reversed the course of his caress. His fingers tested the indentation of her waist for several lazy seconds, then glided upward to linger on the outer curve of her left breast. "I'm not even sure he'd hear his alien alert if it went off."

"His—" Susan's breath caught at the top of her throat "—what?"

"His alien alert," Kyle repeated. "You know he's involved in SETI, don't you? The Search for Extraterrestrial Intelligence?"

Susan bit her lip, distracted by the sensations he was evoking in her body. "Yes," she eventually answered. "He gave Charlie some computer files to take to camp. Something about, uh, radio transmissions, I think."

Kyle nodded. Although his expression was bland, there was a gleam in his heavy-lidded eyes that told Susan he was very much aware of the effect his touch was having on her. She made a silent vow to repay his teasing.

"H.G. believes, as a lot of people do, that if aliens are trying to establish contact with us, they're probably using microwave radiation," he said. "It's the optimum method for galactic communication for a whole slew of reasons. It's fast. It's efficient. And it's probably the best way to cut through all the noise out in space. In any case, H.G. is a member of an ad hoc SETI network that's divvied up the sky—or, at least, the nearest hundred million stars or so—and is listening for radio signals."

"I see." She did, vaguely.

"Ask Charlie to explain it to you sometime," he advised with a smile.

Susan refused to be baited. "What's this 'alien alert'?"

"H.G.'s got a computer program that processes incoming data and weeds out all known artificial and natural radio signals. It's looking for something that *isn't* supposed to be there. Something that's regular, not random. Something that indicates there's an intelligence behind it."

"And if it finds something like that, the alert goes off?"

"Uh-huh. H.G. normally checks the computer printouts a couple of times a day. But when he's writing..." A second smothered yawn.

"He wants to make certain he doesn't miss anything," Susan completed, surprised to find herself genuinely intrigued. She'd never spent much time contemplating the idea of making contact with aliens from outer space.

"Exactly."

Susan began stroking Kyle's chest. "Has the alert ever gone off?"

"False alarms."

"Oh."

"There was *one* unexplained episode. It happened not too long before I came back. H.G. says there were about a dozen reports of UFO sightings that same night. He's halfway convinced he picked up some kind of message."

"Do you believe in UFOs?"

"I don't *not* believe in them."

"When you were a pilot, did you ever—" Susan broke off. She'd never really spoken to Kyle about his flying career.

She watched her lover's lips twist. She saw a shadow enter his eyes. "A couple of close calls," he responded flatly. "But no close encounters."

There was a brief silence.

Susan went back to caressing Kyle's upper body, savoring the contrast between the springy crispness of his tawny chest hair and the resilient smoothness of the skin beneath. She suddenly recalled her earlier determination to give him a taste of his own teasing medicine.

"Have you ever heard your uncle's alien alert?" she eventually asked.

"Just once. He insisted on demonstrating it for me."

"Loud?" Susan deduced from his tone. She began to move her hand lower.

"Like I said," he replied, "it may not be— What are you doing?"

"Nothing," Susan lied sweetly. "Go on. It may not be what?"

"It may not be enough to get through to H.G. if he's caught up in his writing. But it'd probably raise the de— *Susan!*"

A distinctly feminine sense of satisfaction suffused her. "Speaking of raising the dead," she quipped.

Kyle had gone rigid. "There's a difference between being dead and resting, you insatiable little witch."

"Are you saying I tired you out?" She traced the blunt length of his masculinity, feathering her fingers lightly over the tip.

"I'm saying, ah, ah . . ."

"Having trouble thinking?"

"Susan." Kyle spoke through gritted teeth.

"An insufficient supply of blood going to your brain, perhaps?"

"I don't . . . oh, Lord . . ."

"It could be a hormonal imbalance. Or testosterone poisoning."

"*Testosterone poisoning?*"

"You know, I think you were right about the not-being-dead part. I do believe I'm beginning to detect some definite signs of— Oh!"

She'd realized Kyle was quick, of course. And strong. But she'd never anticipated he was capable of reversing their positions with such ruthless alacrity. One instant she had him at her mercy. The next instant she was stretched out flat on her back, pinned down by his weight.

"Better," Kyle announced smugly.

She squirmed. "Let me up."

"Eventually." He began to caress her. "Maybe."

"I don't— Oh. Please. Don't— Oh . . . oh . . ." She arched involuntarily as he finessed a particularly sensitive part of her anatomy.

"Sorry," Kyle apologized after pulse-pounding seconds.

Susan's body was quivering with the sweet aftershocks of the pleasure he'd just triggered. "No, you're not."

"No, I'm not." He winked. "I will be if you want me to, though."

Susan took a deep breath. "What I want is for you to let me up."

"We've already discussed that."

"Well, at least—" Oh, sweet heaven, he was touching her again. How did he— He knew her body better than she did! "Kyle. Please."

"That's my name and that's what I'm trying to do."

"I didn't mean— Oh...yes..." She twisted. "Will you... *stop?*"

He did, his body stiff, his expression concerned. "Are you serious?"

"Just for a minute."

The tension went out of him. "Can I watch the clock?"

"Kyle—"

"Will I get time off for good behavior?"

Susan choked back a laugh. She squirmed once again. "You wouldn't recognize good behavior if it jumped up and bit you on the—"

"Now, now. Watch the language."

"Well, you wouldn't!"

"Probably not. On the other hand, I'm sure I'd recognize *you* if you jumped up and bit me, ahem, just about anywhere."

"In your dreams."

"Funny you should mention my dreams. Why, just the other night—"

"Kyle!"

His mouth curved into a roguish grin. "Your minute is up, Susan."

Afterward Susan came dangerously close to confessing the details of *her* dream involving aluminum foil underwear and a lightning bolt.

"So, what do you think, Susan?" Wendy Marino asked two days later, displaying a photo from a glossy magazine. "It'd be a terrific style on you."

Susan studied the picture. The style in question was an elegant upsweep. It was the kind of coiffure that required four hands, two hours and a degree in structural engineering to do properly.

"It's gorgeous, Wendy," she said. "But it's just not me." She indicated her freshly shampooed hair. "I'm into the long and loose look."

The owner of the Curl Up and Dye Style Salon accepted this rebuff with a shrug that involved more than her shoulders. "Kyle likes your hair down, hmm?"

Susan didn't need to look in a mirror to know she'd started to blush. In point of fact, Kyle *did* like her hair down, something she'd discovered a few days after they'd become lovers.

They'd been lying together in her bed, savoring the aftermath of shared—and satisfied—passions. Kyle had been straining her hair through his fingers in a slow steady rhythm.

"I like your hair this way," he'd murmured.

"Messy?" she'd asked drowsily.

He'd laughed. "No. Down."

"You've never seen it up."

"Yes, I have."

The tone of this assertion had piqued her curiosity. She'd raised herself on one elbow so she could look at him. "When?"

"The night you went out with Jack Wiley."

She'd thought back. She *had* worn her hair up that evening! But Kyle hadn't said a word about it. "I didn't think you'd noticed."

He'd smiled. Slowly. Sensually. "I notice everything about—"

"Susan?"

The sound of Wendy's voice brought Susan back to the present. She scrambled to pick up the thread of their conversation. "Well, yes," she conceded. "Kyle does like my hair down."

"You're not embarrassed by my bringing him up, are you?" the blonde asked. "I mean, it's been kind of obvious what's going on, what with that T-bird of his parked in front of your house every night."

Susan stayed silent. She knew she couldn't argue the point.

"Is he coming by to pick you up?"

"No. He's...gone."

Wendy nearly dropped the comb she'd just picked up. "Gone?"

Susan avoided meeting the other woman's gaze. One of the reasons she'd scheduled this appointment was to keep her mind off Kyle's absence and its implications. "He's in Connecticut. An old commander of his from the Air Force is the head of an aviation-manufacturing firm there. They were supposed to meet about a week and a half ago but something came up."

"This is a job interview?"

"Yes."

"I didn't figure he was going to stay around here all that long."

Susan suppressed a sigh. "Neither did I."

Wendy fell silent after that, devoting herself to the precutting work of sectioning off Susan's hair and pinning it out of the way. Susan glanced around the salon. She wondered how many of the women she was looking at knew where Kyle Gordon had been spending his nights.

The conversation going on at the station next to Wendy's suddenly caught her attention.

"A UFO hunter for the government?" the customer was asking.

"That's what he said," the hairdresser confirmed. "Alfred Petty or something like that. Flashed this fancy ID badge, said he wanted to come in and ask me some questions about that police report I filed back in June."

"The one about the UFO you saw?"

"Uh-huh. My husband said it was a bunch of weather balloons."

"So, did you talk to him? The government investigator, I mean."

"No. I didn't have time. But even if I hadn't been in a rush, I'm not sure I would have let him in. He was kind of strange. Plus, he had the *worst* case of dandruff I've ever seen. Anyway. Let's get you moved over to the dryer, all right?"

"Jack thinks all that UFO stuff is nonsense," Wendy commented.

Susan started. "Jack Wiley?"

Wendy repositioned Susan's head. "Uh-huh."

"I saw the two of you together about a week and a half ago."

"You were out with Kyle, right?" Narrowing her eyes, the blonde began to cut Susan's hair with careful little snips.

"Yes."

"That was my first date with the Wild Man."

Susan jerked, narrowly missing losing a chunk of her earlobe.

"Susan!" Wendy admonished.

"Sorry."

"You went out with him once, didn't you? Jack, I mean."

Susan eyed the scissors. "Yes. I know his sister, Ramona."

"A setup, right?" Wendy sighed. "Those never work for me."

"Do you really call Jack Wiley the, ah, Wild Man, Wendy?"

The beautician stopped cutting. "What do you call him?"

Susan considered for a moment, then told the truth. "Nice."

"Oh—" Wendy shivered voluptuously "—I'd *never* call him that!"

"H.G.?" Kyle called as he opened the front door to his uncle's house. No matter that it was past midnight. The place was unlocked and lit up like a Las Vegas hotel.

His meeting in Connecticut had run much longer than he'd anticipated. He'd gone into the interview believing that pity had prompted his old commander to approach him with a possible employment opportunity. Colonel Jefferson Reid had been grounded ten years earlier because of a heart condition. Kyle had figured that Reid was one of the few people in the world who truly understood how having his wings clipped had affected him.

He'd been right about the understanding. But he'd been totally off target about the pity. He'd been stunned to discover that Reid's interest in him was rooted in bottom-line practicalities.

He'd driven back to Wilder's Forge with a job offer in his pocket, his mood bouncing from one end of the emotional spectrum to the other.

What's the matter, hot dog? the voice inside his skull had inquired, speaking up for the first time in more than a week.

You knew it was going to end. You knew you were going to leave. This job gives you an excuse to—

I don't want an excuse, dammit! Kyle had retorted.

You want to stay in Wilder's Forge—is that it? What would you do? Spend your life giving exhibitions at the local video-game arcade?

What about Susan?

What about her? She knows this thing of yours is short-term. She set the schedule, remember? Charlie comes home the day after tomorrow. Do you think she's going to keep carrying on with you once he's back?

No, he didn't think that. He understood Susan's priorities and where he ranked among them. As he'd told himself nearly two weeks before, he was in her life on a probationary pass, on a temporary basis.

"H.G.?" he called a second time, heading back to his uncle's office.

He found the older man sitting in a swivel chair in front of his word processor. H.G. had the silver Orb in his lap. His eyes were fixed on the computer screen, his fingers were flying over the keyboard.

Smiling, Kyle crossed to stand behind his uncle. He spent about thirty seconds reading the material on the monitor. It was terrific stuff, he decided. Maybe H.G. was right about the Orb stimulating creativity.

After helping himself to a chunk of the cheddar cheese he found in the small refrigerator sitting next to H.G.'s desk, Kyle prowled around the office. Although most of the cartons had disappeared, many of the items they'd contained, including his old BB gun, were still lying around.

The flashing light on H.G.'s answering machine caught his attention. Kyle glanced at his uncle, then moved to the machine and hit the rewind button.

He went through about twenty minutes' worth of stuff before hitting something that sent a nasty sensation crawling up his spine.

"Mr. Gordon, this is Alvin Pettit," an adenoidal voice declared. "I need to talk to you. It's very important. I'll call again."

Kyle hit the forward button after the click of disconnection. A minute later he found another message from Alvin Pettit. A minute after that, two more. Finally:

"Mr. Gordon, it's 11:37 p.m. on Wednesday. This is Alvin Pettit. I know you're there. Why won't you pick up? I'm not going to go away, Mr. Gordon. I know you've made contact. It's not fair of you to keep it a secret! Please. Just talk to me. Tell me. I've waited my whole life for something like this!"

Kyle pressed the stop button and checked his watch. Assuming Alvin had been telling the truth, that message had been left ninety minutes ago.

"H.G.," he said sharply.

No response.

Impelled by an anxiety he couldn't explain, Kyle crossed to his uncle in three lithe strides. Grasping the older man by the shoulders, he turned him away from the keyboard and monitor.

The Orb rolled off his uncle's lap. H.G. blinked like a man awakening from a trance. "Kyle!" he said, smiling. "Nice to see you again."

"Never mind that," Kyle snapped. "Has Alvin Pettit been here?"

H.G. looked puzzled. "I don't know. Has he?"

Kyle thrust a hand through his hair. "There are a whole bunch of messages from him on your answering machine. The last one sounds pretty strange. Pettit accuses you of making contact and keeping it a secret."

"Contact? What kind of contact is he talking about?"

"That's what I'd like to know. When was the last time you left the house, H.G.?"

The older man frowned. "I'm not really certain. I've been so caught up in my writing the past week or so—"

"Have you seen anyone recently? Spoken to anyone?"

"Just you, Kyle. You know the way I get when I'm on deadline."

"Yeah. I know." Kyle glanced around, mentally replaying Alvin Pettit's last phone message. The guy had definitely sounded weird.

"Do you mind if I go back to my book?" his uncle inquired hopefully. "I was just starting the climactic battle scene."

"No, of course not." Kyle decided there was no point in pursuing the matter of Alvin Pettit with his uncle. "Sorry to disturb you."

"No problem." H.G. swiveled around and started writing again.

Kyle let a few moments go by, debating what to do next. Finally he moved back to the answering machine. Flicking off the recording mechanism, he picked up the phone and punched out a series of numbers.

A click of connection. One ring. Two rings.

"Seven-seven-seven-five. Williams. Talk to me." The voice on the other end of the line was all business.

"Leroy? Kyle Gordon."

"Gordo, my man!" The change of tone was dramatic. "Long time no hear from. How's it hangin'?"

"Kind of low and heavy, buddy," Kyle admitted frankly. "Look, I'm sorry to bother you at home—"

"It's cool."

"I need some information."

"If it's not classified and I've got it, it's all yours."

"You work with Alvin Pettit, don't you?"

"Not anymore. He up and quit about...hmm. Lemme think. Jeez. Well, not to bring up a sore subject, but old Alvin said adios, muchachos, a couple of weeks after your accident. There's no connection. That's just the time frame I remember."

Kyle felt the skin on the nape of his neck tighten. "Did he give a reason for his resignation?"

"Nope. Not that anybody asked. They were too glad to see him go."

"I've heard he was difficult."

"Understatement of the year. I mean, Alvin was always a little far out. But the last few months before he left... I tell you, Gordo, the guy was beyond freaking Pluto. What's your interest in him?"

Kyle glanced over at H.G., who appeared to be totally absorbed in his writing. "He's been bothering my uncle."

"Bothering your— Wait a minute. H. G. Gordon? The sci-fi king?"

"That's right."

"Man, I love his stuff! He lives in the Hudson Valley, right? Some little place—Wilber's Fence?"

"Wilder's Forge. That's where I am now."

"Mmm. Well, it makes sense. Alvin bugging your uncle, I mean. First of all, there's the sci-fi angle. Second of all, there's the Hudson Valley connection. Alvin's got a real interest in the UFO sighting reports coming out of that area. And third of all, he's hung up on this, uh, Wilder's Forge. Claims the locals are covering up alien contacts."

"*What?*"

"I've only heard bits and pieces of this, you understand. But Dr. Pettit apparently put together a device that detects some special kind of low-level, electromagnetic anomaly. And this device evidently registered two of these anomalies in your uncle's hometown. He says it's the find of the century. Everybody who's seen his data says it's a load of crap."

"Do you think he's dangerous?"

"Well, that breath of his is pretty toxic."

"I'm serious, Leroy."

A pause. Then, "No. I don't think he's dangerous."

"You're sure?"

"As sure as anybody can be about anybody else. Yeah, the guy is as obnoxious as a boil on the butt, but I've never picked up any indication he's a menace to society. Does that ease your obviously troubled mind?"

"Yeah. It does," Kyle replied. "Thanks. I owe you."

"No prob."

They talked casually for another few minutes, covering a wide variety of topics. Among them, the job offer Kyle had had from Jefferson Reid.

"Well, gotta go, Gordo," Leroy said eventually.

"Sure." While Kyle still harbored a few concerns about Alvin Pettit, his anxiety was much less acute than it had been. "Thanks again."

"Hey, man, you've done me plenty of favors in the past. Just one thing, though."

"Yeah?"

"Let's hope that if there *are* aliens running around Wilder's Forge, they never meet up with Dr. Pettit. He'd give them a real negative impression of the human race, know what I mean?"

Kyle chuckled ruefully. "I think I've got a pretty good idea. Then again, there's probably a lot of folks who fall into that category."

It was a perfect night for a picnic. The sky was cloudless, the weather calm and clear. Susan was glad. She desperately wanted this, probably her last night alone with Kyle, to be flawless.

"More?" she asked, gesturing to the goodie-laden basket on her right.

Kyle, who was lying with his head in her lap, gave her a lazy smile. "I have everything I need right now, thanks."

The answer was perfectly innocuous, of course. Still, Susan found herself flinching inwardly at it. She couldn't help wishing that the man she loved so dearly could, indeed, have everything he needed. Because if he did, he might not leave Wilder's Forge.

She took a sip from the glass of champagne she was holding, praying her face didn't betray the longing welling up within her. As the bubbles from the wine danced against her tongue, she reflected on the singular inappropriateness of the beverage she'd selected. Champagne was a symbol of celebration. Yet the last thing she felt like doing was celebrating.

She took another sip, studying Kyle. He seemed relaxed. His expression, clearly illuminated by the trio of small kerosene lamps they'd brought with them to their picnic site on the edge of Cumming's Meadow, was reflective.

She closed her eyes for a moment, bracing herself against a sense of impending loss so painful it almost deprived her of the ability to breathe. The fact that this loss was something she'd expected, something she'd *accepted,* didn't ease the hurt.

She opened her eyes once again. Twelve days, she thought. Just twelve days...

Her feelings for Kyle had been intense from the start. But they'd increased in vibrancy and depth since she'd faced their true nature. The more she'd learned about the man who had claimed her heart, the stronger her love for him had become.

No, Kyle wasn't perfect. He could be stubborn, self-centered and short-tempered. He'd been endowed with an overabundance of charm, and he had no compunction about taking advantage of it. He was not, by his own brash admission, a "nice" person.

Still, none of his flaws detracted from the fact that he was the most compelling man Susan had ever known. He could have her sputtering with outrage one second and melting with ecstasy the next. Even at his worst, he seemed to bring out the best in her—a best no one else inspired.

There'd been moments during the past twelve days when she'd wondered how long she could go on hiding her emotions from him. There'd been moments, too, when she'd wondered how Kyle could be so utterly attuned to some of her feelings and so totally oblivious to others.

Sometimes all it took was a teasing word or a brushing touch to bring her, trembling, to the brink of a confession. She'd been on the verge of crying out her love for him more times than she wanted to count.

She hadn't cried it out, of course. She hadn't cried it out because, as she'd told Kyle the morning after they'd first made love, she wasn't a twenty-one-year-old girl who still believed in happily-ever-after endings.

Yes, she sensed fundamental changes in Kyle since the day Charlie had brought them together in the video-game arcade. And yes, she thought some of these changes were due to her and her son. But when it came to the possibility that a blue sky guy who was obviously in search of himself could be transformed into a man who was prepared to commit to love and marriage and fatherhood ...

No. That sort of transformation was the stuff of fairy tales, and Susan knew it.

She drank the remainder of her champagne and put the glass down. Time to face reality, she told herself.

"You know, I've been thinking about your job offer from Colonel Reid," she commented. Kyle had detailed the results of his interview earlier.

Kyle gave her an odd look. A lock of hair had flopped down over his forehead. He forked it back in the careless gesture that had become heartbreakingly familiar to Susan during the past weeks. "Have you?"

"It sounds like a great opportunity."

"I suppose."

"You don't see it that way?"

He shrugged. "I spent thirty years of my life picturing myself doing one thing. Working for Colonel Reid wasn't it. I guess I'm still trying to readjust my vision."

Susan worried her lower lip for a few seconds, plucking at the skirt of her gauzy cotton dress. "How old were you the first time you flew?" she finally asked, broaching a subject she'd always steered away from around Kyle.

His mouth quirked. "Six weeks."

"What?"

The quirk became a curve. His dimples appeared. "My dad was reassigned right after I was born. We flew from his old base to the new one."

"Oh."

"I was five the first time I touched the controls on a plane. My dad took me up in a trainer a couple of months before he and my mom were killed. He strapped me into the copilot's seat and told me I could help him fly. It was . . . Lord . . . I can't describe it exactly. But the instant I laid my hands on the yoke, I knew it was going to be my life. H.G. gave me flying lessons for my twelfth birthday. I was a full-fledged aviation junkie by that time." He laughed, a hint of ruefulness entering his expression. "You knew Miss Stacia, didn't you? She taught English at the high school for about a century."

"Mmm. She retired a few years ago."

"Yeah, well, I had her for senior English. One of the assignments she gave us was to write a poem. I wrote one about flying. *She* thought it was about sex. She was all set to have me suspended until H.G. intervened and explained the, uh, facts of life to her."

"That sounds like Miss Stacia." Given the passion she heard in Kyle's voice when he spoke about flying, Susan could understand why there had been a mix-up.

There was a small break in their conversation then. After a few moments, Susan shifted her position. The stray lock of hair had fallen over Kyle's brow again. She brushed it back into place.

"Do you have reservations about Colonel Reid's offer because it involves aviation?" she questioned.

"Aviation is what I know, Susan."

"But to be around planes and not be able to..."

His eyes met hers. The intensity of his gaze made Susan stop speaking. "It won't be any harder than seeing the sky every day," he said.

Susan drew a shaky breath. She'd long since noticed Kyle's habit of scanning the sky. "What...what do you see when you look up at the sky?" It seemed desperately important that she know.

Kyle lifted his gaze to the heavens. The glow from the kerosene lamps did nothing to soften the starkness of his expression. Susan waited tensely, watching the small muscles of his jaw quilt.

"I see a place I want to go that I can't get to anymore," came the devastatingly simple reply. "I see...somebody else's future."

Susan's heart lurched. She whispered his name.

For a single pulsing moment, everything seemed to stop.

Then he moved. A split second later, so did she. Suddenly they were lying together on the picnic blanket they'd spread on the ground several hours earlier.

Their mouths mated in a long, liquid kiss. Susan opened her lips, welcoming the slick sweep of Kyle's tongue. She invited. Enticed. Incited.

"Yes," she murmured. "Oh...yes..."

The flavor of him flooded Susan's tongue as the kiss became more intense, more intimate. She breathed in deeply, inhaling the musky scent of Kyle's masculine arousal and the clean fragrance of the meadow around them.

"Susan...oh, Susan..." His voice was husky. Almost hoarse. He nuzzled at the right corner of her mouth, then nibbled along the ripe curve of her lower lip to nuzzle at the left. His tongue came in search of hers once again. She responded with a throaty sigh.

His hands moved over her body, mapping the lines, mastering the curves, making Susan dizzyingly aware of her femininity. He touched. She trembled. The heat of his palms and fingers seemed to burn straight through the fabric of her clothes. She felt her skin flush and grow feverish.

She nipped at his lips as though sampling some exotic tidbit, then planted a line of brief brushing kisses along his jaw. A hint of new beard growth abraded her mouth.

Susan tugged the T-shirt he was wearing free of the waistband of his jeans. Pulling the garment up, she began to caress him with slow, savoring strokes. She relished every tremor of response she felt, every shuddery gasp she heard.

She combed her fingers through the crisp mat of his chest hair with great delicacy, then traced his nipples with teasing deliberation. Kyle growled like a jungle cat.

There was a row of buttons running up the bodice of her dress. They were undone almost before Susan became aware of what was happening. The tiny clasp that held her bra closed gave way next.

She quivered as Kyle cupped her newly bared breasts. He brushed his thumbs back and forth over her nipples, transforming them from plush crests to pebble-hard buds.

"Beautiful," he praised. "So... beautiful..."

Susan was never certain which of them removed her panties or which of them unzipped his jeans. Such details and distinctions had ceased to matter long before she felt the tantalizing search of Kyle's clever fingers between her thighs. She cried out when he touched her, muscles deep within her body spasming in response to a pleasure so intense it was perilously close to pain. He touched again, urging her closer and closer to the brink of fulfillment.

"With you... Kyle..." she pleaded. What was the use of ecstasy if she experienced it alone?

His hands glided up to clasp her waist. He shifted his leanly powerful body in a single sinuous movement. A moment later, he was on his back and Susan was straddling him.

"I'm...with you," he told her thickly. The glow from the lamps burnished his face, underscoring both the virile strength and the potent sensuality of his compelling features. His brows were drawn together in a V and the tanned skin of his cheeks was pulled tight.

Emboldened as never before, Susan bent forward to kiss him. His hands came up to cover her breasts as she did. The languid stroke of his fingers against her sensitive flesh was an erotic counterpoint to the hurried marriage of their mouths.

Finally the clamor for consummation became too demanding to be ignored. Susan knelt up, poising herself like a tightrope walker. Kyle clasped her hips, his fingers flexing.

"Yes," he urged fiercely.

Trembling with eagerness, yet trying to prolong the experience, Susan took Kyle within her body. She sheathed him by hot, honey-sweet increments.

Aching...inch by inch. Melting...moment by moment.

She felt the first convulsive tremor of her release a few seconds after their joining was complete. She felt Kyle shudder at the same time. Looking down, she saw he was staring up at the night sky.

"*Fly...with...me!*" she gasped.

They soared, together.

They touched the stars the same way.

Ten

——

"What do you think about Hotdog?" Charlie asked three days later.

"Hot dog?" Kyle repeated, stiffening. He slanted a glance to his right, then returned his gaze to the road ahead. It was shortly before dusk. He and Charlie were driving home from a "guys only" day trip to Bear Mountain State Park. They were now approaching the outskirts of Wilder's Forge.

"Yeah. As a name for the puppy I'm going to get."

Kyle relaxed. What had he thought? he wondered, mocking himself. That the kid had been tuning in on the voice inside his skull?

"It'd certainly be different, Charlie," he observed.

"But cool, right?"

"Oh, absolutely."

"I couldn't believe it when Mom told me she'd been thinkin' about my writin' I wanted a pet and that she'd decided I could get a puppy. Boy. I'm really glad I didn't bring that rat home." There was a pause. Then, "Did you tell her about that, Kyle? The rat, I mean."

Kyle kept his eyes on the road. "I mentioned it, yeah."

"I figured. I guess she knows about the explosion, too, huh."

"Has she said anything?"

"No. But she checked out my face really intensely when she came to camp to pick me up on Friday."

"Well . . ."

"It's okay if you told her, Kyle."

"Actually, she knew something was up even before I did, buddy. She was very suspicious of that letter you wrote to her."

"But . . . I made everything sound great!"

"Too great. She decided you were hiding something."

"Jeez." Charlie was obviously both impressed and appalled by his mother's perceptivity. Then, "Do they look okay? My eyebrows, I mean."

Kyle glanced to his right again. Charlie had removed his glasses and turned to face him. "They look fine to me," he said honestly.

There was a brief pause.

"Did I tell you Mom called that guy in the paper?" Charlie asked after a few moments. "The one who put in the ad about the puppies?"

Kyle shook his head. He knew about the ad. He'd shown it to Susan.

"The guy said we can come by anytime and check them out. But we have to wait a couple of weeks before we can take one home." The boy sighed sadly.

"A couple of weeks isn't that long, Charlie."

"Yeah, but you're probably going to be gone by then, right?"

Kyle tightened his grip on the T-bird's steering wheel. "Probably."

"Do you *really* have to leave?"

"Yeah, kid. I do."

"It's because of that job you're getting in Connecticut, huh?"

"I need to make a living." The response was accurate but evasive. There was no way he could explain the reasons he was leaving to Susan's ten-year-old son. In fact, there were moments when he wasn't sure he could explain them to himself. All he knew for certain was that he couldn't stay.

"How come you can't make a living in Wilder's Forge?"

"There's nothing I can do there."

Not for the first time, Kyle wondered whether he'd be so determined to leave Wilder's Forge if Susan gave him a sign—any sign at all—that she wanted him to stay. Maybe. Maybe not. That was another thing he wasn't sure of. The point was, she hadn't given him a sign. And he'd watched for one. God knew, he'd watched for one.

Which was pretty perverse, when he considered it. Because if Susan *did* give him a sign, if she *did* hint that she wanted more from their involvement, it probably would scare the living daylights out of him.

It's better this way, he told himself. You and Susan had something special. It was terrific while it lasted. But now it's over.

He'd screw things up if he stuck around. Despite his many other uncertainties, Kyle was positive about this. While he truly believed he'd changed since his return to Wilder's Forge, he wasn't going to delude himself that he'd changed *that* much.

As for the possibility of his asking Susan to go with him when he left Wilder's Forge...

There was no way it could work. Because asking her to go with him would mean proposing marriage, and that was something he wasn't ready for. Hell, he wasn't really ready for this new job he was taking!

Susan understood what a good marriage was. She'd had one with Mike. If he thought he could offer her that...

But he couldn't. He knew it. She knew it.

"You *are* going to come back, right?" Charlie queried anxiously. "Like, to visit H.G. and me and Mom and stuff?"

Kyle switched on the T-bird's headlights. It seemed to have gotten much darker in the past few minutes. "Sure."

"You're not just saying that, are you?"

Kyle winced inwardly, knowing that he'd spent nearly all his adult life "just saying" things. Not lying, exactly. But being...careless about the truth. He'd invested his integrity in his flying. He'd played fast and loose with just about everything else.

You're right not to trust me, kid, he thought. *I* don't even trust me anymore.

"No," he replied. "I'm not just saying that. I promise I'll come back to visit. I can't tell you when. But I will come back."

"I'm going to miss you a lot, Kyle."

"I'm going to miss you a lot, too, Charlie."

"I think Mom's going to be sad when you go."

Kyle said nothing. He knew Charlie was aware that he and Susan had "gone out on dates" during the past two weeks. What he didn't know was how the boy interpreted this. For all his scientific sophistication, Charlie still had a very simple view of male-female relations. Kyle was not going to be the one to complicate this outlook. Time—sooner or later, for better or worse—would take care of that.

They stayed silent for several minutes. Finally Charlie spoke up again. "Do we have time to go by H.G.'s house?" he asked hopefully. "I know Mom's expectin' us for dinner. But like I told you this morning, I brought a copy of the report we did at camp on searching for aliens. He's probably thought of all the ideas we came up with. Still . . ."

Kyle consulted the dashboard clock. "We're running a little ahead of schedule," he said. "And I'm sure H.G. will be pleased to get your report."

Five minutes later, he turned onto the road that led to H.G.'s house and nearly ran head-on into another car. He didn't have time to think. He just reacted. Turning the T-bird's steering wheel, he swung wide and narrowly averted a collision. The other vehicle, which was speeding with its headlights off, didn't even slow down.

Kyle cursed. "What the hell kind of idiot—?"

"Jeez!" Charlie cried simultaneously. He sounded more excited than upset. "That guy drives even faster than *you* used to!"

Kyle spent the next minute or so concentrating on getting himself and his devastatingly candid young passenger to H.G.'s place in one piece.

"Look," Charlie said as they parked. "The front door's open."

"Yeah, kid." Kyle unbuckled his seat belt as he surveyed his uncle's house. The skin on the back of his neck prickled. "I see."

"Do you think . . ."

"I don't know what to think." Kyle debated silently for a few moments. He was faced with two bad choices. He didn't want to bring Charlie inside with him. Yet he couldn't very well leave him sitting alone in the car, either. If anything happened to him . . .

"Kyle—"

He cut the boy off with a gesture. "Look. We're going to go in together. I want you to stay right behind me and I want you to keep absolutely quiet. If I tell you to get out, I want you to run like hell. You don't argue. You don't look back. Do you understand me, Charlie?"

Charlie nodded. "Yes—" he gulped "—sir."

"Okay. Move out."

They came to a halt a few steps inside H.G.'s front door. Kyle watched and waited. Listened and looked.

Nothing.

"H.G.?" he finally called.

No response.

"H.G.?"

Still no answer.

Kyle glanced down at Susan's son. Charlie was staring up at him, clearly waiting for guidance. The youngster's eyes were wide and round behind the lenses of his glasses. His freckled cheeks were pale.

"We're going to head to H.G.'s office," Kyle told him quietly. "Remember what I said."

The kid nodded once again, his Adam's apple bobbing.

Kyle made certain Charlie stayed directly behind him every step of the way. He was also certain to block the boy's view when he paused in the doorway of H.G.'s office and looked in.

"Oh, no," he whispered.

His uncle was sprawled on the floor, unconscious. The pieces of some sort of electronic device lay strewn around him.

Kyle reached H.G. in five fast strides and hunkered down beside him. He shed some of the soul-chilling anxiety he was feeling when he saw the older man was breathing. He searched for a pulse. . . .

Strong and steady. Thank God. Oh, thank God.

"Is he . . . is he d-dead?" Charlie asked in a hushed, scared-sounding voice. He'd come to stand next to Kyle.

Kyle glanced up at the boy, offering him a reassuring smile. "No, buddy. He's not dead. I think he must have—"

He broke off as his uncle moaned and stirred.

"H.G.?"

"Ohhh . . ."

"H.G., it's Kyle. It's all right. You're safe."

Another stirring movement. Another moan. A moment later, Kyle saw H.G.'s eyelids twitch, then flutter upward.

"Wh-what—?"

"Easy. It's okay, H.G. Everything's okay."

"Kyle?" H.G. blinked, obviously confused. "Ch-Charlie?"

"I was afraid you were d-dead." Charlie sank to his knees.

The older man smiled crookedly. "Not . . . quite," he answered, struggling to sit up.

"Easy," Kyle said once again, slipping a supportive arm around his uncle's shoulders. "What happened?"

The smile vanished. "It was Alvin Pettit."

Kyle ground his teeth. Dammit! He'd had a bad feeling about Pettit. Why hadn't he listened to his instincts?

"Who's Alvin Pettit?" Charlie wanted to know.

"He hunts UFOs for the government—" H.G. began.

"*What?*" Charlie's voice jumped about an octave.

"Not anymore, he doesn't," Kyle interrupted. "He quit his job."

"Did this UFO guy break in and attack you, H.G.?"

"Not exactly, Charlie." H.G. gave Kyle an apologetic look. "All those times you warned me about locking the house . . ."

"Water under the bridge," Kyle said dismissively. "What happened?"

H.G. took a moment to collect his thoughts. "Well, I was working on my book," he began. "I was putting the finishing touches on a scene when I heard this odd sound. I looked up and there was Alvin Pettit. He was standing next to my desk. He had a device in his hands. It had blinking lights. It was buzzing. He told me it detected, ah, ah . . . I can't quite—"

"Electromagnetic anomalies," Kyle filled in flatly.

H.G.'s brows soared. "Yes. That's it! But how . . . ?"

"It's not important. Just go on with your story."

"He, Dr. Pettit, said his device had detected two of these, ah, anomalies in Wilder's Forge and that one of them was in this house. He said these anomalies were caused by . . . alien artifacts. He accused me of leading a conspiracy to prevent him from finding out about contacts with sentient beings from other planets. He was very upset. He set the device down and he grabbed me. I fought back. Somehow the device got knocked over and smashed. We struggled again. I think I lost my footing. I remember falling. I must have hit my head on something and knocked myself unconscious."

"How do you feel?" Kyle scrutinized his uncle's face. H.G. was a little paler than usual, but that was to be expected. His eyes were clear and the pupils seemed to be reacting normally. The account he'd just finished delivering had been reassuringly coherent and concise. Even so . . .

"My head hurts a bit and I'm a little shaky," the older man admitted. "But I don't think I sustained any permanent damage. Do you suppose you could help me to my feet?"

"Okay," Kyle agreed, knowing his uncle was going to attempt to stand with or without assistance. "But we're going to take it nice and slow."

"We have to call the police," Charlie stated, lending a hand.

"We will, buddy," Kyle promised, keeping a firm grip on his uncle.

"Do you think this Alvin guy stole anything?"

The older man glanced around in response to Charlie's question. "It's difficult for me to tell. I don't—" Suddenly he froze.

"What?" Kyle asked, alarmed.

H.G. looked at him. "Your BB gun." He inclined his head. "It was right over there."

Kyle exhaled. "Forget that. The damned thing doesn't work."

"But, Kyle—"

"Forget it, H.G.!"

"All right," the older man said. He looked around a bit more, his brow furrowing. "I don't . . . I don't see the Orb."

"The Orb?" Charlie repeated. "What's . . . the Orb?"

"Actually, Charlie, it's something you might be interested in seeing," H.G. answered. "It's this very unusual— Oh! Thank heavens. There it is." The older man pointed.

Charlie turned his head. Kyle heard him gasp.

"It's just like my Bliss Ball," the boy said in an astonished voice.

Something inside Kyle went cold. His mind flashed back to the day Charlie had gone off to science camp.

"You keep that Bliss Ball out of your luggage, young man!" Susan had called as they'd watched Charlie run back to the house to get his gear.

"Bliss Ball?" he'd echoed. "What's a Bliss Ball?"

"Just this—" she'd sketched a spherical shape about the size of a canteloupe with her hands "—thing Charlie picked up someplace. . . ."

Kyle felt the muscles of his body clench. He said Charlie's name.

The boy turned back to face him, obviously wary of his tone.

"Do you have—" Kyle gestured toward the Orb "—one of those?"

Charlie nodded. "I found it in Cumming's Meadow. A couple of weeks before I met you." The boy looked at H.G. "Where did you get yours?"

"Oh, it's not mine," H.G. said simply. "It's Kyle's. He found his in Cumming's Meadow, too. He was about your age at the time."

Charlie's eyes slewed back toward Kyle. "Really?"

Kyle didn't reply. "Do you know anybody else who has a Bliss Ball?"

"No." An emphatic shake of the head. "I showed it to the guys at school. They thought it was cool. They would've said if they had one, too."

"Where's yours right now?"

"In my room, under my bed. I saw it this morning when I was looking for my sneakers. I don't know how it got—Kyle?"

Kyle didn't respond. Pivoting, he crossed to the telephone, snatched up the receiver and punched out Susan's number.

One ring. Two mysterious silver spheres found in the same secluded meadow years apart, he thought.

Two rings. One apparent lunatic making claims about alien encounters and electromagnetic anomalies.

Three rings. It couldn't be . . . could it?

Four rings. Kyle closed his eyes for a moment. Answer, Susan, he begged silently. Please, answer. Let me know you're all right.

Five rings. Then six. And seven. And eight.

"Kyle."

Kyle opened his eyes and looked at his uncle. It was obvious H.G. had come to the same conclusion he had.

He hung up the phone and focused on Susan's son. "Charlie," he said steadily, "I want you to stay here. I've got something I have to do."

"What?" Charlie demanded.

"I'll tell you after I get back."

Kyle could practically hear the click of connection in the kid's clever brain. "You think this Alvin guy is after Mom, don't you!" Charlie accused. "And it has something to do with the Bliss Ball. *My* Bliss Ball!"

"Charlie—"

The boy shook his head. "I'm not staying here."

"Charlie—"

"*No!* She's my mom, Kyle! I'm *not* going to stay here! I'll run after you if you leave me!"

Kyle didn't doubt Charlie for an instant. "All right," he capitulated. "But it'll be just like before. You'll do every single thing I tell you to do. No back talk. No balking."

Charlie nodded solemnly.

Kyle looked at his uncle again. "H.G., I want you to call the police and explain what happened here. Tell them to get out to Susan's house. But for God's sake, tell them *not* to come in with lights blazing and sirens blaring. If Pettit's there, I don't want him spooked."

"Will do," his uncle agreed.

"Pick up the . . . whatever that thing is and move out, Charlie."

Fifteen seconds later, they were sitting in the T-bird. Kyle fished the car key out of the pocket of his windbreaker. As he thrust the key into the ignition, he glanced to his right. "Fasten your seat belt, son," he ordered.

Charlie stopped stroking the silver sphere in his lap and gasped. "Wh-what?"

Kyle started the engine, lead-footing the gas pedal to hide the shock he was feeling. "Just buckle up," he rephrased gruffly. "We've got to go save your mom."

An instant later, a raise-the-dead klaxon started sounding inside H.G.'s house.

Charlie practically jumped out of his skin. "What's that?"

Kyle put the T-bird into reverse. "It's my uncle's alien alert."

If it hadn't been for her fear of what he might do to Charlie or Kyle, Susan probably would have felt sorry for Dr. Alvin Pettit.

He was unappealing to the point of being pathetic. Short. Stoop-shouldered. Whey-faced and miserably myopic to judge by the thickness of the lenses of his taped-together glasses. He was also, as she'd overheard at the Curl Up and Dye Style Salon only days before, suffering from one of the worst cases of dandruff in history.

He'd appeared at her house roughly fifteen minutes before. The instant she'd started to open the door—a stupid thing to do, she now acknowledged—he'd pushed his way inside and pulled a gun. Then he'd begun raving about alien artifacts and electromagnetic anomalies, about close encounters and conspiracies.

There'd been a moment or so when he'd seemed to be winding down. Unfortunately the sudden shrill of the telephone had set him off again.

Listening to those eight rings had been agony for Susan. She'd known, absolutely, positively known, that the person on the other end of the line was Kyle. She'd *felt* him urging her to pick up the receiver. She'd *heard* him pleading for her to answer and assure him she was all right.

She estimated that five minutes had elapsed since that call. Although Pettit's manner was still unnervingly itchy-twitchy, his mood appeared to have calmed. He'd finally stopped pacing and perched himself on a chair set several feet to the left of the sofa where she was sitting.

Susan examined her intruder and the gun he was holding. Maybe she could try. . . reasoning with him, she thought.

"Why are you looking at me like that?" Alvin demanded.

"I'm sorry," Susan apologized. "Dr. Pettit, I'd like to help you. If you'll just tell me what it is you're looking for—"

"I don't *know* what I'm looking for! If I still had my anomaly detector I could find it. But H. G. Gordon destroyed it!"

Susan's mouth and throat went dry. "You've seen H.G.?"

Alvin squirmed. "Yes."

"Before you came here?"

"Y-yes."

Susan swallowed hard. "Did you...do something to him?"

Alvin's eyes scuttled back and forth behind his glasses. "I'm not sure."

"Dr. Pettit—"

A lightning-swift change of mood. "It's all his fault! *He's* the mastermind behind all this. He and that nephew of his!"

"Kyle?"

"Oh, don't pretend you don't know! You think I haven't kept track of you two? That story about him being washed out of the air force—hah! It's all a hoax so he could come back here and help cover up the alien contacts. And you're helping him!"

"No!"

"Yes!" Alvin insisted furiously. Suddenly the anger seemed to go out of him. He slumped. "Why won't you tell me?" he asked, his expression pleading. "I— Okay. Okay. I know I haven't handled this very well. I don't have very good people skills. I realize that. I've tried to work on it. But, w-well, there's so much else about m-me that n-needs fixing...."

For a moment, Susan thought he was going to cry. "Dr. Pettit—"

"Please." He leaned forward. "Please, Mrs. Brooks. Just show it to me. Let me look at it. Maybe...t-touch it."

Susan gestured helplessly. "I would if I knew what it was. Believe me. I can see this means a lot to you—"

"Everything!" Alvin corrected wildly, his mood changing once again. "It means everything to me! I dreamed of being an astronaut, you know. But by the time I got to high school, I realized I'd never qualify. So I decided to devote myself to the Search for Extraterrestrial Intelligence. And I have. Only people are shutting me out of the truth! And I'm not going to stand for it anymore! Do you hear me, Mrs. Brooks? I'm not going to—"

He broke off, sitting bolt upright, his head swinging toward the living-room picture window. *"What's that?"* he demanded.

Susan didn't answer. But she could have. Because *that* was the sound of Kyle's Thunderbird pulling up in front of her house.

"That's the car, Kyle!" Charlie pointed to the vehicle parked in the driveway of his house. "That's the car that almost ran us over!"

"It sure is, kid," Kyle affirmed tightly. He set the T-bird's brake, undid his seat belt, then turned. "Are you straight about our plan?"

The boy nodded. He was clutching the Orb to his chest.

Kyle eyed the gleaming silver sphere for a moment. He'd reached over and laid his palm against it once during the wild drive from H.G.'s house. Something inexplicable had happened. The icy knot of fear twisting in his gut had eased. The anger he'd felt toward Alvin Pettit had dissolved into pity. He'd suddenly known that everything was going to work out as it should.

But then he'd lifted his palm and the fear and the anger had returned. His certainty about what was going to happen had disappeared.

"Kyle?" Charlie asked.

Kyle stripped off his windbreaker. "Here," he said, handing it over. "Wrap the Orb, uh, Bliss Ball in this."

The boy did as he'd been bidden, swaddling the metal globe in the garment's dark material. "Done."

"Okay. Let's go."

They got out of the car and marched up to the front door. Kyle kept one step ahead of Charlie all the way. He rang the bell.

After several nearly unendurable seconds, the door swung open to reveal Susan. Alvin Pettit had her positioned in front of him like a shield. Her face was pale and her eyes were dark and wide. Kyle saw her lips move once. There was no doubt they were shaping his name. Then Susan's gaze flicked down and she registered Charlie's presence. What little color she had left in her cheeks drained away.

It was, Kyle acknowledged later, one hell of a time for a man to realize he'd fallen in love with a woman, but that's exactly what happened to him during those first few moments of confrontation. The truth about the emotion he'd variously classified as lust and want and need clouted him on the head and clutched him by the heart.

For a split second he felt the way he'd felt in the wake of his accident. Dizzy. Disoriented. No longer in control. And then the world seemed to realign itself. What had been shattered was reassembled. What had been wrong was suddenly made right.

He loved her. *He loved Susan Brooks!*

"It's all right, Susan," he said huskily, taking a step forward.

"I have a gun, Major Gordon!" Alvin declared. "I have a gun and I . . . I won't h-hesitate to use it!"

Kyle froze in midstride. If his hunch about Alvin's "gun" was correct, the threat was an empty one. But if it wasn't . . .

He couldn't chance it. Not here. Not now.

"Come into the house and close the door," Alvin ordered.

Kyle obeyed. Charlie followed, still holding the cloth-covered Orb.

There was a tense silence. Kyle forced himself to focus exclusively on Alvin. It was very difficult. Every cell of his brain and body was clamoring for him to look at Susan.

It's going to be all right, love, he thought. *I promise you. Everything's going to be fine.*

He eyed the handgun Alvin was clutching. He was almost positive it was his old BB pistol. But there was something slightly... off about it.

If he'd been alone, *almost positive* would have been enough. He would have trusted his own agility and strength and made a grab for the gun. But he wasn't alone and that made all the difference in the world.

"We've got what you want, Dr. Pettit," he said evenly.

Alvin stiffened. "What?"

"Alien artifacts. Two of them. One's right here." He indicated the bundle Charlie was holding.

"Let me—" Alvin gulped "—see it."

Kyle glanced at Charlie and nodded. The boy unwrapped the Orb. Kyle heard Susan catch her breath.

"That can't— It looks like a giant ball bearing!" Alvin protested.

"What did you expect?" Charlie challenged. "A 'Made on Mars' label?"

"Charlie!" Both Kyle and Susan spoke at exactly the same time, with similar urgency.

Amazingly the boy's sarcasm seemed to get through to Alvin. For a moment, Kyle actually thought the scientist looked embarrassed.

"No. No, of course not," Alvin muttered. Then he looked at Kyle again. "You said *two* artifacts. Where's the other one?"

"You'll have to let Charlie go get it."

Alvin shook his head vehemently, creating a flurry of dandruff.

"Oh, come on," Charlie said disgustedly. Kyle wondered whether the influence of the Orb—assuming there really was any influence—had completely short-circuited the kid's ability to perceive danger. "I'm not going to hurt anything. I'm only a kid! You've got my mom. *And* a gun."

Again, Charlie's comments seemed to hit home with Alvin.

"All right," he assented, gesturing with the pistol.

Charlie handed the Orb to Kyle and dashed out of the room.

"Why did you bring him here, Kyle?" Susan asked an instant later.

Kyle looked at her then, struggling to resist the sudden calm that threatened to blunt the edge of his resolve. "I didn't have any other choice," he answered. "I knew you wouldn't... be..."

His voice tailed off. His heart was thudding, his pulse thrumming. He would have sworn he felt the Orb pulse against his palms.

He wanted to tell Susan he loved her. More than anything else, he wanted to take her in his arms and tell her how dear she was to him. And once he'd done that...

He saw Susan's expression change. Her lips parted. A hint of astonishment sheened in her brown eyes. Color blossomed in her cheeks.

"Stop that!" Alvin commanded shrilly. "Stop looking at each other—"

"Got it!" Charlie announced, racing back into the room.

There was another silence. Kyle watched Alvin's gaze bounce back and forth between the two spheres. Questioning. Coveting. After a few seconds there was an audible change in the scientist's breathing pattern.

"Roll them over here," he ordered, licking his lips.

Kyle and Charlie complied. The Orb and the Bliss Ball came to a halt a few inches from the toes of Alvin's badly scuffed shoes.

"All right." Alvin nodded. He seemed to have trouble getting his head to stop moving. "Mrs. Brooks. You pick them up and give them to me."

Kyle watched as Susan did as she'd been instructed. He saw a tremor run through her when she retrieved the second sphere.

"Here, Dr. Pettit," she said softly. "Here's what you... need."

Kyle fully intended to jump Alvin the second Susan stepped back. He figured there was no way the other man could handle the two metallic globes *and* a weapon. He was poised for the strike when—

Alvin dropped the gun. He dropped it, and the damned thing fired when it hit the floor. A lamp sitting on a table on the opposite side of the room shattered.

Charlie yelped. Susan gasped. Kyle cursed in disbelief.

Alvin fainted. He clutched the Orb and the Bliss Ball to his chest, gave what sounded a lot like a moan of ecstasy and crumpled into an unmoving heap.

Kyle surged forward, kicking the gun away. Then he bent and checked Alvin. Pulse: strong. Respiration: steady. Overall condition: out cold.

Kyle straightened. Like iron to a magnet, his gaze went to Susan.

Blue eyes met brown across a distance of no more than eight feet. Kyle felt his heart skip a beat.

He said Susan's name in a wondering whisper.

She said his in the same way.

And then, all at once, she was in his arms.

"Susan...Susan...Susan..." he said, raining kisses on her brow, her cheeks, her nose and her lips. "Oh, sweetheart. Oh, love."

She pulled back, quivering. "Wh-what did you call me?"

"Love," he repeated fiercely. "I love you, Susan. I . . . love . . . you."

"R-really? You . . . you're not just saying—"

He claimed her lips with a deep kiss. "No," he assured her hoarsely. "I'm not just saying that. I *love* you, Susan. I know I can't offer you—"

This time *she* silenced *him* with a kiss. "There isn't anything I want in this world that you can't give me, Kyle Gordon," she said, her eyes filling with tears. "I . . . oh, I love you, too!"

"Aw, Mom," Charlie protested, "don't start crying!"

Kyle and Susan broke apart. Kyle felt himself flush. "Buddy..."

Susan opened her arms to her son. "Charlie, I'm not crying because I'm sad or scared. I'm crying because I'm happy."

Charlie moved forward. "Because Kyle said he loves you?"

"Yes, honey," Susan said, hugging him. She smiled tenderly at Kyle.

"Jeez." Charlie squirmed. "I could've told you that weeks ago!"

Kyle almost choked. "Well, I wish you'd clued me in!"

Charlie pulled away from Susan and gave him an indignant look. "I *did!* Don't you remember? I *said* you were lookin' at her all goony—"

Ding-dong.

Everyone froze. After a moment Kyle crossed to the front door and yanked it open. He expected to find police officers. What he saw was his uncle. The older man's blue eyes were blazing. His rotund body was quaking.

"Aliens," H.G. gasped. "Aliens—in Cumming's Meadow."

Eleven

Susan's memory of the drive to Cumming's Meadow was always pretty much of a blur. All she could recall were fragments.

A piece of a volatile exchange between Kyle and his uncle:

"You *fixed* it?" the man she loved and who loved her back yelled over his shoulder. "You *fixed* my BB pistol and you didn't tell me?"

"I *tried* to tell you, Kyle!" H.G. shouted from the back seat of the Thunderbird. "Don't you remember? Earlier? Back at the house? But you wouldn't let me."

The moment she took her first and last look at the car's speedometer:

"Omigod!" she gasped, not wanting to believe her eyes. She'd known the Thunderbird was fast, but this was insane!

Kyle glanced over at her. "Don't worry, sweetheart," he said, winking. "All four wheels are still on the road."

Nonetheless, she felt a definite deceleration a few seconds later.

Oddly enough, her most vivid recollection was of something Alvin Pettit said to her son. Pettit had regained consciousness while H.G. was in the midst of elaborating on his extraordinary announcement. He'd immediately begun begging to be taken to the rendezvous site. They'd ended up bundling him— and the Orb and the Bliss Ball—into the back seat of the T-bird.

They'd just swung onto the access road that led to Cumming's Meadow when Charlie, who was tucked between her and Kyle, asked in a tremulous voice, "What if...what if these aliens really do come and they're like the Embols, Kyle? You know. The evil alien invaders in the v-video game?"

Susan covered her son's hand and gave it a reassuring squeeze. She saw Kyle glance right and open his mouth. But before he had a chance to respond to Charlie's anxious question, Alvin spoke up.

"Don't be afraid, Charlie," he said serenely. "The beings who made these spheres are bound to be kind and good."

Alvin's words were still echoing in Susan's mind a short time later when she stood on the edge of Cumming's Meadow—not far from the spot where she and Kyle had made love—and stared up at something she'd never truly believed existed.

It was an aircraft of some sort. She had the impression it was huge. The structure was difficult to discern, but it was solid and it blotted out a big piece of the night sky. The UFO was V-shaped and studded with bright white lights. It hovered silently.

For a few moments, Susan was absolutely terrified. "Kyle," she whispered shakily, "are y-you seeing . . . ?"

Kyle was standing to her right. She felt his arm slip around her waist. He drew her close. "Yes. I'm seeing it, too."

Charlie was standing to her left. He took her hand. "It's okay, Mom," he said. "They won't hurt us."

The lights flickered suddenly. They changed from white to green, then back to white again. From somewhere behind her, Susan heard H. G. Gordon utter the word "incredible."

The lights changed colors again. Their configuration seemed to alter. They pulsed from blindingly brilliant to barely perceptible.

Out of the corner of one eye, Susan saw Alvin Pettit, still clutching the Orb and the Bliss Ball, fall to his knees. She understood how he felt.

Suddenly all the lights seemed to merge. A shimmering column of blue-violet illumination spilled to the ground. And standing in the center of the column . . .

Gasps from the two people she loved most in the world told Susan that if she was hallucinating, she was not doing so alone.

"What do you see, Susan?" Kyle asked hoarsely.

"One...being," she answered. Somewhere in the back of her mind she realized that the terror she'd felt a short time ago had totally evaporated. "Tall. Thin. Two arms and two legs. A big bald head. Two huge eyes."

"Me, too." Kyle sounded relieved. "Small mouth and ears. Skin—"

Suddenly, Susan heard the Being speak. Not aloud. But inside her head. A strange tingle danced through her nervous system. She swayed.

"Greetings to you."

"Greetings," chorused Kyle, Charlie and H.G.

"Oh, greetings!" cried Alvin Pettit.

"Uh, uh, g-greetings," Susan managed to stammer.

"Please. Do not fear us. We mean no harm."

"You come in peace, right?" Charlie prompted.

"Yes. We come in peace. But with a purpose."

Kyle let go of Susan and took a step forward. His militarily correct posture projected an unshakable combination of assurance and respect.

"Is this purpose to reclaim lost property?" he asked.

"Yes." The Being gestured toward Alvin Pettit. *"Two Keepers."*

"Why do you call them 'keepers'?"

"We assign Keepers to our little ones," came the explanation. *"The Keepers provide both protection and companionship. They tend to the little ones' needs and fulfill their wants— when it is fitting."*

"You mean they're like alien baby-sitters?" Charlie sounded stunned.

Susan was ready to swear she felt a tickle of extraterrestrial laughter inside her brain.

"Yes," the Being agreed. *"And like you, Charlie, our little ones are not always pleased that their elders believe they need watching over."*

Charlie gasped.

"How did the two Keepers end up in Cumming's Meadow?" Kyle wanted to know.

"We visit your planet from time to time. And because we wish our little ones to learn as much as possible about the wondrous variations of life, we have brought them—and their Keepers—with us. Unfortunately it is the nature of little ones to be..." The Being hesitated, as though searching for a word.

"Careless?" Susan suggested. "Are you saying your little ones lose things?"

"Exactly. When it was discovered that the first Keeper had been left behind, we decided it would be less risky to replace than retrieve."

"And when you found out about the second missing Keeper?" H.G. asked. "The one Charlie found?"

"There was only a little concern at first. But then..."

"But then what?" Kyle pressed.

"The Keepers are linked. Resonations from them are picked up by all. We began detecting certain... disruptions. We ultimately realized it must be due to the two lost Keepers. We feared the consequences."

"So you signaled you were returning to Earth in hopes the right people would pick up your message," H.G. said.

"Yes."

"Are you going to take the Bliss Balls away, then?" Charlie asked.

"We must," the Being said simply, and gestured toward Alvin Pettit.

Susan turned her head at the same time Kyle and Charlie did. She gasped at the same time they did, too. The silver spheres the scientist had been clutching so frantically simply disappeared.

"No!" Alvin stared at his suddenly empty hands. "Please, don't!"

"We're sorry," the Being declared gravely.

There was a pause. For the next few seconds, the only sounds Susan heard were the whistle of the night wind, the hoot of an owl and the sobs of Alvin Pettit.

"Can't you let him keep one of them?" Kyle demanded, taking a step forward. "Dammit, there must be some way you can unlink—"

"No," the Being said. "Although it is generous of you to ask. To have compassion for one who has wronged you is a noble thing."

"Look, I don't care much about nobility—"

"We understand that, Kyle Gordon. What you care about is the sky."

Susan felt her heart skip a beat. It had been one thing to hear the Being address Charlie by name. She'd sensed a kind of parental indulgence when that had happened. But this was different. The Being seemed to be speaking to Kyle as an equal. Or at least as a kindred spirit.

"What do you mean?" Kyle asked, taking another step nearer the column of light. Susan bit her lip, willing him not to move again.

"We know you, Kyle Gordon. You are like us. You are a seeker after stars. One who dreams of the gift of flight."

"Mom," Charlie whispered, "I'm starting to get scared."

"It's all right, honey," Susan whispered back, steeling herself against a sudden weakness in her knees. "It's all right."

"You know what I was," Kyle said. Susan could hear the strain in his voice. She could see the tension in his shoulders. "Not what I am."

"You have been damaged," came the thoughtful assessment.

"Yeah, right." Kyle gestured. "Damaged. Permanently."

"Very little is . . . permanent."

Without warning, a pale blue aura appeared around Kyle's skull. Susan cried out in alarm as she saw the man she loved go rigid. She tried to rush to his aid, but she couldn't seem to move.

"Mom!" Charlie exclaimed.

"Kyle!" H.G. shouted.

They, too, seemed rooted to where they were standing.

Then, just as suddenly as it had appeared, the light around Kyle's skull vanished. He staggered, his movements clumsy and uncoordinated.

Susan discovered she'd regained the ability to move. She ran to Kyle's side. "Kyle. Oh, God. Are you all right?"

He stopped staggering. He gripped her arm, steadying himself. She stared up into his compelling face. "Kyle?" she repeated desperately.

He blinked rapidly several times. His grip on her eased. After a moment he let go of her entirely. Susan watched fearfully as he lifted his right hand and pressed it against his ear for a few seconds. Once he lowered his hand, he shook his head as though trying to jar something loose.

"Kyle?" Susan whispered.

He looked at her, eyes blazing. "Susan. Susan...I think..."

"Do not think, Kyle Gordon," the Being counseled. *"Know. What has been damaged is now repaired."*

Kyle pivoted to face the column of light.

"Come with us, Kyle Gordon," the Being invited. *"The sky is yours once again. Come fly with us."*

There was a pause. Susan closed her eyes for a moment, biting the inside of her cheek so hard she drew blood. She remembered the pledge she'd made to herself the morning after her first night with Kyle Gordon.

She'd promised that when he left, as she knew he ultimately would, she'd kiss him goodbye, wish him Godspeed and let him go.

She opened her eyes, drawing herself up and cocking her chin. "Kyle," she said.

He turned toward her. His expression was impossible to decipher.

"Say yes," she told him. "Say yes and go with them. They'll take you to all the places you thought you couldn't get to." She swallowed, willing herself not to cry. "It's your dream, Kyle. Your future. Claim it."

Kyle Lochner Gordon hadn't known until that moment how deeply Susan Eleanor Brooks loved him. Nor, in truth, how deeply he loved her.

The heedless, blue sky guy he'd been for far too many years would have accepted the carte blanche she was offering. The man he'd finally become didn't even consider it.

"No, Susan," he answered. "You're my future. You. And Charlie. And maybe a baby or two down the road. That's my dream, sweetheart. And whether or not I'm able to fly again—" he brought his hands up to cup her face, using the pads of his thumbs to brush away the silvery tears that had begun to roll down her soft cheeks "—when I'm with you, love, I soar."

He embraced Susan even more fiercely than he had when he'd confessed his love for the first time. After several incandescently happy seconds, he turned slightly and extended an arm toward Charlie. The boy ran to him. They hugged. Then Charlie hugged Susan. Finally the three of them faced the Being... together. As a family.

"*You wish to stay?*" Kyle sensed a hint of approval in the question.

"More than anything in the universe," he answered.

"Ahem."

It was H.G. With one arm still around Susan, Kyle turned.

"If I might make a suggestion," his uncle said, addressing the Being. "Why don't you take Dr. Pettit with you?"

Kyle's eyes snapped toward the scientist. Alvin was still on his knees on the ground. At the mention of his name, his head came up.

"M-m-me?" he stammered. "M-me go into... space?"

"*Well... ah...*" The Being was clearly taken aback.

Alvin stumbled to his feet. He sniveled, then wiped his nose with the back of his hand. "Why not m-me?" he questioned. "I don't mind not being your first choice. I don't mind if I'm your last choice!" He started to walk forward, his eyes fixed on the column of light. "I know what I'm like. I'm not very attractive. And I'm psychologically maladjusted. Plus my personal hygiene isn't that great. But I'm all alone in the world. I could disappear off the face of the Earth and no one would miss me. Actually, a lot of people would be glad to see me go. So, please. If you'd just look into my heart and mind, you'd see! You'd see that I have dreams about space, too. All my life...more than anything else...please. Take me. Oh, please..."

The Being gestured. A split second later, Alvin Pettit's entire body was enveloped in a shimmering blue-violet glow. Kyle's skull tingled.

"My God," Susan whispered.

"Extraordinary," H.G. murmured.

"Awesome," Charlie said.

The glow finally faded away. The Alvin Pettit who emerged stood straight, had no dandruff on his narrow shoulders and, to judge by the haste with which he discarded his glasses, probably possessed twenty-twenty vision.

"Oh, thank you! Thank you!" Alvin cried. "What did you do?"

"We did as you asked. We looked into your heart and mind."

"Does that mean...?"

"The choice is yours, Alvin Pettit. Will you fly with us?"

"Yes!"

"Then join us."

Alvin moved forward. Just before stepping into the column of light, he turned. "Goodbye!" he called, and snapped off a salute at Kyle.

Something more powerful than military training prompted Kyle to return the gesture.

A moment later, Alvin and the Being were gone. A moment after that, there was nothing in the sky but twinkling stars and a silvery half-moon.

"Jeez!" Charlie gasped.

"Jeez, indeed," H.G. concurred.

"What do you see now?" Kyle heard Susan ask.

He stared at the sky for three or four seconds. "The beginning of the rest of my life," he finally responded, then lowered his gaze to meet hers. "And it looks absolutely beautiful."

One month later, Susan Eleanor Brooks Gordon lay in bed with her new husband, the recently reinstated Major Kyle Lochner Gordon, USAF. They'd been married eight hours earlier in Wilder's Forge. Charlie had given the bride away.

H.G., who was going to be looking after Charlie for the next week, had been best man.

"Kyle?"

"Mmm?"

"Do you think we did the right thing?"

Kyle levered himself up on one elbow. "If you're having second thoughts, Susan, forget them. We're married. You're mine for life."

"I'm not talking about that." Susan laughed. She reached up and traced the line of his jaw. "I was wondering if we did the right thing in not telling anyone about our close encounter."

Kyle's brows went up. "It was H.G.'s idea. And if *he* believes keeping quiet is the best approach . . ."

"I know. It's just that . . ."

"You have a secret yen to wind up on the cover of a tabloid?"

"No."

"You wanted to spend our honeymoon being interrogated about what really happened to Alvin Pettit?"

"Of course not!"

"Sweetheart." Kyle leaned in and kissed her. "The information will get to the right people at the right time. I promise you."

There was a short pause.

"Speaking of Alvin . . ."

"Do we have to?"

"I just wondered if you thought he was happy."

"Offhand, I'd say he's the second-happiest guy in the universe."

"The second?"

"Mmm-hmm."

"Who's the first?"

"No idea?"

"Well, I wouldn't want to make any immodest assumptions."

"Feel free to make anything you want. Immodest assumptions. Improper suggestions. Immoral advances. Anything."

Susan spent the next ten minutes taking her new husband at his word. It was difficult to tell which of them enjoyed the experience more.

Afterward, she brought up a subject she knew Kyle had avoided as assiduously as she had the previous four weeks.

"Kyle?"

"Not again. Not yet. I need some rest, Susan."

She smothered a laugh. "You're lying in a bed with a woman who loves you. What could be more restful than that, darling?"

Once again, Kyle propped himself up on one elbow. His hair was thoroughly mussed, his eyes half-hidden by his lids. A flush rode high on his cheekbones. He looked slightly debauched and devilishly attractive.

"What could be more restful?" he countered mockingly. "How about a fifty-mile forced march with a rucksack full of rocks?"

"What a charming thing to say to your new bride."

"You're lucky I have the energy to say *anything* to you at this point." He began to caress her. "What was it you wanted to talk about?"

Susan twisted, her pulse scrambling at his touch. "Talk?"

"I assume that's why you said my name a minute ago."

"Oh." Susan tried to rake her thoughts together. "Yes. It...it's about the Orb and the Bliss Ball."

For a moment, she thought Kyle might make a joke. Then he nodded, his expression turning reflective. His hand stilled. "I know, love."

"It's just that...you found yours, you wanted a friend, and Mike's family moved to Wilder's Forge. Charlie found his, he wanted a father, and *you* came to town. Then *I* found Charlie's Bliss Ball—"

"And you wound up with a quart of mint-chocolate-chip ice cream," Kyle interpolated wryly. "Susan, don't you think I've wondered about this as much as you have? Yes. I believe it's possible the Keepers had an influence on our lives. But when it comes to what you and I have together now—what we're going to have for the rest of our lives—that's *us*, love. That's a matter of two human beings who've committed to each other. It's got *nothing* to do with alien artifacts.''

"Oh . . . Kyle . . ." Susan sighed, happily surrendering to the long, languid kiss her husband used to underscore his assertion.

"Speaking about artifacts," Kyle said eventually.

"Were we . . . speaking?" Susan teased.

"Occasionally. In between the nonverbal communicating."

"Ah."

"I've got a wedding present for you. From Ramona Bozeman. She said you'd explain it to me."

"What?"

Kyle repeated his previous statement as he got out of bed.

"Kyle?" Susan questioned, sitting up. Despite her puzzlement, she couldn't help savoring the sight of her husband's naked body.

"Back in a flash," he promised over his shoulder, then disappeared into the bathroom and shut the door.

"Kyle?" Susan called a few seconds later. "Why would Ramona give *you* a wedding present for *me*?"

The bathroom door swung open. Kyle stepped out. "I think that's one of the things you're supposed to explain."

Susan gawked. No, she thought. No. Ramona wouldn't do this to me!

But Ramona had.

Kyle was no longer naked. He'd donned a pair of briefs. The briefs were skimpy and silver and emblazoned with a bolt of lightning.

Susan felt herself begin to blush. In the space of two or three heartbeats, her entire body was suffused with heat.

"I understand there's supposed to be a crash helmet and cape with this," Kyle commented mildly. "They wouldn't fit in my shaving kit."

Susan tried to say something. Nothing came out.

"Could you at least give me a hint about the lightning bolts?"

"Bolts . . . plural?"

"Mmm. Front and back." He demonstrated.

"I . . . I . . ."

"Yes?"

Susan drew a deep breath. "It's not something I can explain, Kyle."

"No?"

"I'd rather . . . demonstrate. If you know what I mean."

Kyle switched on the Gordon Grin, upping the wattage as high as it would go. He moved toward his new wife. "I haven't got the slightest idea what you mean, Susan," he replied huskily. "But I'd sure like to find out."

Hours later, Kyle Lochner Gordon heard from the voice inside his skull for what his instincts told him was the very last time.

You're A-OK, hot dog, was all it said.

*   *   *   *   *

SILHOUETTE® Desire™
MAN OF THE MONTH

YOU'VE ASKED FOR IT, YOU'VE GOT IT! MAN OF THE MONTH: 1992

ONLY FROM SILHOUETTE DESIRE

You just couldn't get enough of them, those men from Silhouette Desire—twelve sinfully sexy, delightfully devilish heroes. Some will make you sweat, some will make you sigh . . . but every long, lean one of them will have you swooning. So here they are, *more* of the men we couldn't resist bringing to you for one more year. . . .

BEST MAN FOR THE JOB
by Dixie Browning in June

MIDNIGHT RIDER
by Cait London in July

CONVENIENT HUSBAND
by Joan Hohl in August

NAVARRONE
by Helen R. Myers in September

A MAN OF HONOR
by Paula Detmer Riggs in October

BLUE SKY GUY
by Carole Buck in November

IT HAD TO BE YOU
by Jennifer Greene in December

Don't let these men get away! MAN OF THE MONTH, only in Silhouette Desire!

MOM92JD

VOWS
A series celebrating marriage
by Sherryl Woods

To Love, Honor and Cherish—these were the words that three generations of Halloran men promised their women they'd live by. But these vows made in love are each challenged by the tests of time....

In October—Jason Halloran meets his match in *Love* #769;
In November—Kevin Halloran rediscovers love—with his wife—in *Honor* #775;
In December—Brandon Halloran rekindles an old flame in *Cherish* #781.

These three stirring tales are coming down the aisle toward you—only from Silhouette Special Edition!

presents
SONS OF TEXAS
by Annette Broadrick

As rugged as their native land, the Callaway brothers—Cole, Cameron and Cody—are three sinfully sexy heroes ready to ride into your heart.

In September—
LOVE TEXAS STYLE! (SD#734)

In October—
COURTSHIP TEXAS STYLE! (SD#739)

In November—
MARRIAGE TEXAS STYLE! (SD#745)

Don't let these Sons of Texas get away—men as hot as the Texas sun they toil... and *romance*... under! Only from Silhouette Desire...

Take 4 bestselling love stories FREE
Plus get a FREE surprise gift!

SILHOUETTE® Desire™

**Beginning in August
From
Silhouette Desire
Lass Small's
Fabulous Brown Brothers**

When the Brown Brothers are good, they're very, very good.
But when they're bad...they are fabulous!

Read about Creighton, Mike and Rod in Lass Small's upcoming
Fabulous Brown Brothers series. And see if you don't agree.

In August—A RESTLESS MAN (SD #731)
In October—TWO HALVES (SD #743)
In December—BEWARE OF WIDOWS (SD #755)

Boys will be boys...and these men are no exception!

Silhouette

CHRISTMAS
Stories 1992

Experience the beauty of Yuletide romance with Silhouette Christmas Stories 1992—a collection of heartwarming stories by favorite Silhouette authors.

JONI'S MAGIC by Mary Lynn Baxter
HEARTS OF HOPE by Sondra Stanford
THE NIGHT SANTA CLAUS RETURNED by Marie Ferrarrella
BASKET OF LOVE by Jeanne Stephens

Also available this year are three popular early editions of Silhouette Christmas Stories—1986, 1987 and 1988. Look for these and you'll be well on your way to a complete collection of the best in holiday romance.

Plus, as an added bonus, you can receive a FREE keepsake Christmas ornament. Just collect four proofs of purchase from any November or December 1992 Harlequin or Silhouette series novels, or from any Harlequin or Silhouette Christmas collection, and receive a beautiful dated brass Christmas candle ornament.

Mail this certificate along with four (4) proof-of-purchase coupons, plus $1.50 postage and handling (check or money order—do not send cash), payable to Silhouette Books, to: **In the U.S.:** P.O. Box 9057, Buffalo, NY 14269-9057; **In Canada:** P.O. Box 622, Fort Erie, Ontario, L2A 5X3.

ONE PROOF OF PURCHASE	Name: _____
	_____
	Address: _____
	_____
	City: _____
	State/Province: _____
SX92POP	Zip/Postal Code: _____

093 KAG